The Pig Heiress

H. Marie Indigo

H. Marie Indigo

The Pig Heiress

Copyright © 2024 by H. Marie Indigo

All rights reserved.

First published in 2024

ISBN (paperback): 979-8-9898243-3-5

ISBN (ebook): 979-8-9898243-2-8

Contents

To all the cats. Pspsps.

Chapter One

The glazed ham leaves a brown streak on my plate as it slides into the smaller bowl next to mine. I don't eat pigs. My older brother, Patrick, on the other hand, has eaten a lot of them. My older sister, Belle, only ate one her entire life before she died just after I was born, and that was only because Patrick tricked her into doing so when they were kids.

My parents must eat them all the time, but I can't remember a time in the eighteen years I've been alive when I even saw them for a meal. They're always working at our family's pig farm, Swiney Acres, and aren't around much. Brandon and Tilda Florence are only home between sunset and sunrise, and then it's only to fulfill the most basic of parental duties and to drop off a day's supply of pork products.

To be fair, their absence is utterly perfect because I can push off the thick slabs of bacon and meaty pork chops onto my surviving sister, Mary's, plate. She's barely six years old and hasn't learned yet to tattle, so I usually get away with it.

But not tonight.

No, definitely not tonight.

Patrick is at the table and the vibe he's giving could literally sing to the skies about how unhappy he is with me right now. I could almost see the unpleasantness bubbling like hog fat beneath his skin and he's just waiting until I'm done chewing the food in my mouth before he can lay into me with his harsh words. And I know they will be harsh because if there is anything you should know about the Florence family, it's that we like to speak our minds.

"You're an ungrateful little wretch, do you know that?" He starts, refusing to even look in my direction and instead concentrating on his own food. Mary giggles beside us and chews absently on my discarded pork.

Maybe when she's older, I'll explain to her why I don't eat meat and that, perhaps, she shouldn't either. But considering I saw my innocent and flawless little sister eating a fistful of mud the other day, that talk might not come for a while.

Now Patrick, solidly built and stupid Patrick, is another story. Being the heir to the family's farm, he had it in his mind that every one of us should be one hundred percent dedicated to the craft of pig culling and selling. Meaning we should eat pork all day, every day. No amount of pleading or debating with him could change his attitude. Believe me, I've tried. Nothing could change this stubborn brute's mind.

"I've told you. I won't eat anything that once had a heartbeat," I say back to him. Mary giggles again, but I have no idea why.

"This is our family's legacy, our heritage! You should be..."

"Should be what? Like you? I don't think so!" I slam my hand on the table so hard it stings, a habit I've been trying to break. It causes a nearby glass of water to topple over and Mary laughs with a mouthful of food. Small bits of spit-up ham sprinkle the table in front of us making me sick to my stomach. I try not to look at them and focus instead on the large engagement ring on my finger.

It's too loose and bothering me, so I spin it around between my knuckles.

"Just wait till I tell mother and father about it," Patrick shoots back, frowning deeply and rising from the table.

I don't want to be the one left behind with Mary, even though I know Hildy, our family's nanny, will be arriving soon to take care of her, so I also jump to my feet quickly. I lurch towards the door and put on a satisfying and dashing smile on my face as I turn to smirk at Patrick. He's a few steps behind me and knows he'll need to stay there with Mary until someone comes in to watch her.

After Belle died, our parents weren't going to take any chances with the safety of their remaining female heirs, um, children. Even if that meant Mary and I could ever be alone and had to be shadowed everywhere we went, even within the safety of our own home.

This is why I knew that just outside the dining room door, my own so-called shadowy protector, Milo Shaw, was waiting for me.

The Shaw family has been friends and protectors of the Florence family for generations and it's been so long that I don't think either family remembers how it started. Milo and I have known each other for most of our lives and our parents assigned him as my bodyguard since we were already inseparable. But he'll be out of a job once I'm married off into another family. Then it will be up to my new husband to provide such protections, that is, if he even wants to. No one protects Patrick. The value in my life is that someone can marry into the pig empire, Patrick is destined to inherit it no matter what, with or without a wife. And little Mary is young enough to just have Hildy to watch over her.

"You can tell them anything you want," I yell back at Patrick. "It's not like they care about what I do. I won't be their problem for much longer anyway." The words feel like they wound me more so than him and the engagement ring feels heavy against my fair skin.

I can hear his huffing and puffing as he gathers his strength to tell me again what he thinks of me, but the door closes on his face and I run down the hallway, narrowly avoiding Hildy as she bustles around a corner. I think she says something to me, but I'm too quick for her remarks, and make it outside without her, or anyone else from the estate following me. Everyone that is, except Milo.

His heavy footsteps are behind me as I dart behind the tall hedges surrounding the back gardens and I catch quick flashes of his black clothes as I dart around the well-sculpted statues of various trees. Unlike their real versions, these leafy clunkers are cemented hard into the ground to keep from blowing away in any of the city's many dusty and random storms.

I charge my way through them with Milo hot on my heels but accidentally graze the side of my arm against a low-slung, stoney branch and the swear words pour from my mouth without mercy as I slow my pace and press my fingers gingerly into bruised flesh.

"Classy," says Milo, stopping just out of reach. He's learned over our years together that I can be quite unpredictable. One too many punches to his well-muscled chest have taught him to be careful.

"Milo," I begin, looking up at him. The hazardous run through the stone trees has zapped my energy and a painful stitch in my side has taken over my feelings, leaving me deflated and hungry. "Am I really ungrateful?"

"No," he says simply, leaning against one of the fake trees. "Not really, but I know you well enough to act like you are when you're hungry. Did you eat enough today?"

I run a hand over my stomach in thought and when I look back at him, I can see the troubled look in his eyes.

"I guess I haven't. The cooks here, well, they don't believe in my food choices, you know? Either that or Patrick has paid them off."

Milo chuckles and it's a wonderful sound.

"Come on then, let's go to town and get you something plant-based to eat," he says, gesturing the way out the closest gate and we're soon leaving the garden of still and silent trees behind.

The air is uncommonly still for this time of year, but I feel like it's only just saving its strength for a bigger windstorm soon to come. And while my large home surrounded by its stone guardians might be the safest place to be when it does come, I itch to get away and leave it behind in the night. Even if it's just for the evening.

The Florence family lives in the second largest house in Pioneer Springs. The biggest one belongs to the Lester family. They own the only chicken farm in the area and as everyone around here knows, chicken is slightly more profitable than pork.

Unless you consider cow meat. Beef is expensive stuff! Pricey, luxurious, delicious, or so they say, and highly illegal. Cows have been endangered and protected since the Dusting sixty years ago, which decimated a third of the country's homes, cities, and farmlands, leaving the entire middle part of the country uninhabitable due to the sheer number of natural disasters happening there daily.

Chickens and most breeds of pig were easy enough to keep plump and plentiful for the meat industry, but the cows that hadn't starved to death got very, very lucky when beef was forcibly removed from everyday diets.

Pioneer Springs is actually very close to the border between the civilized West and the area now known as The Dusting. Sometimes during sunrise, I could see the brown swirling void that I knew was that giant, empty, and wild space. I could only see it from the roof of Swiney Acres, though, and most of the time Milo wouldn't let me up there.

For safety, he swore, but I think it's because we would be so alone and isolated on the roof, and he wouldn't want anyone noticing. He's been engaged to a girl named Tasha for almost a year now and always hates the gossipy rumors that seem to plague his relationship with me, even if it is a paid internship.

We've been together almost every day since we were both ten years old and I've cherished every moment of having my best friend always by my side. I don't mind that people, especially his prissy fiancée, question what goes on between us, but I guess he does. His is also an arranged marriage of convenience just as my own because in approximately two weeks, I'm set to become Mrs. Bluebell Lester and the other half of a mighty and powerful chicken-pig empire.

And it really boils my blood to think about it. So, I don't. That is unless the heavy ring on my finger reminds me of my impending fate.

Like right now, I am simply trying to forget, but the unfortunate part is that in order to get into town, we have to pass directly in front of the grand chicken manor itself and I run the risk of Robbie Lester noticing I'm nearby.

"Maybe we can go the back way?" Milo suggests when he notices my hesitation. "The way we used to go to school?"

"No, the only other way now is the Bleached Fields and I think they're still haunted. Patrick had the shorter routes blocked off so he could keep better tabs on me."

"Well, you are the next in line to the pig factory," Milo says with a sly grin.

"Don't remind me." I laugh, playfully shoving him aside. "But maybe if I was in control, I could make some changes. You know, just open the doors and set the pigs free in the wilds. Let nature decide their fates and not some sharpened machinery."

Milo is quiet at my comments as we continue walking down the nicely kept sidewalks. The Western country we're in might be stressed from the number of people now packed into it, but enough money could buy you an abundance of seclusion and all the privacy you could ever want.

I think we're just about to make it to the main road when someone yells from behind us and I turn around slowly to see Robbie's tall form coming at us from the double doorway of his mansion. He doesn't have an escort. He doesn't need one. Anyone brave, or stupid enough, to get on his bad side has either ended up in the hospital or was never seen again.

I used to ask questions about him, especially after my parents so casually announced our engagement when they came home one night, but I never received any answers. The Lesters, it seemed, keep their secrets well.

"Where are you off to, my little sugar plum?" Robbie croons, placing himself directly in my path. I notice him eyeing my left hand as he speaks to me, probably checking to make sure I'm wearing my engagement ring.

"Just going into town to visit a friend," I say, keeping my head high. I refuse to cower in front of him, even if his actual presence makes my skin crawl. I know he can't really hurt me. I'm too important.

Milo, hanging back a respectable distance behind us, clears his throat before asking, "Will you be accompanying us, Master Lester?"

"What?" Robbie looks over, seemingly just noticing Milo's equally tall form. "Um, no. I'd rather not. I have some friends coming over."

Robbie may be bulky with the kinds of muscle that come from eating too much animal protein, but I know Milo could hold his own against him. I've punched him enough in the shoulders to feel how much muscle he has hidden under his dark suits. Still, Robbie is intimidating and I'm glad that after a sloppy kiss to the side of my cheek, he leaves us alone and ventures back into his big house.

I don't wait for Milo to catch up as I start walking as quickly as possible to the main road. Knowing he is at least several paces behind gives me just enough time to let a few tears fall. And there are just enough moments left to wipe them from my face before we come across the first few homes scattered about the center of Pioneer Springs.

"Bluebell," Milo says coming to stand by my side. "Are you okay?"

"I'm fine, really," I tell him and twirl my ring. "Everything is utterly divine."

"I know it isn't," he persists. He takes a few big strides forward on his long legs until he is directly in front of me. Similar to Robbie, he's large and tall in front of me and I feel like a child even though we're the same age. But unlike Robbie, there is kindness and deep, deep caring in his blue eyes.

I used to see longing there as well, but he won't let that show again. Not after what happened when I first noticed it last summer.

"I just..." I stammer, looking for the words I know are there, but refuse to come out. "I used to be able to imagine what my future life would be like, but now it's all blank and just nothing, nothing and nothing. I can't imagine being married to Robbie and I don't even want to think about what it would be like. It sounds so boring."

"He can't be that bad, your brother likes him," Milo says.

"Patrick only likes him for what he'll bring to the family name. He likes him for his chickens and for his money."

"Maybe you can like him for his chickens, too?" Milo grimaces at his own comment and I can tell he'd take it back if he could.

"I want to love someone for who they are and I want them to love me for who I am, even if I'm an ungrateful wretch who won't eat meat. I want to be respected and admired for my own accomplishments, not for being the shoulder someone steps on to climb a throne."

"A throne made of chickens and pigs?"

"Exactly! And ew, gross," I say, nudging him hard with my shoulder. There is no way I could actually move him, but he goes along with it and staggers to the side of the road as if mortally wounded.

I'm laughing at his antics just as the street lights begin to pop on one by one, bathing the sidewalks in a soft, golden glow. I could almost imagine that it was just the two of us taking a walk after dinner. The stars burn above us, those that aren't clouded by the thin layer of dust drifting in from the Dusting, and it's so picturesque and beautiful and perfect all at the same time.

I want to close my eyes and savor it, but I can't. My thoughts are just farfetched dreams that I force myself to close off and put away. I shove them back into the deepness of my mind because things, especially things with Milo, will never be that simple.

Chapter Two

Pioneer Springs is an old town that was established well before The Dusting forced so many people to relocate into the area. Used at first as a resting place for the great migration, most just passed through while on their way to the western coast.

But when the steady pilgrimage declined, more and more people just stayed where they ended up, and soon, Pioneer Springs was a sprawling city just outside the border of the desolate and wasted lands beyond. Well, as sprawling as any city could be after such a muddled time in history. It's still not a very big place and almost everyone knows each other from either school or work at one of the meat factories.

Milo and I continue the rest of our walk along the glowing sidewalks in comfortable silence until the town proper comes into view and the growling of my stomach is so loud he bursts into equally loud laughter.

"So where to, Mrs. Soon-to-be-Lester?" Milo asks, clasping his hands behind his back and walking in step with me.

"Yuck, don't call me that and you already know where we're going, so I don't know why you even ask."

Milo grins but keeps his eyes forward and doesn't respond.

We soon arrive at Sparrow's Books, Coffee and Tea, a small coffee shop connected to an even smaller bookstore. My other best friend, Flame, works here as part of her Required Industry Service. A program installed by the government requires everyone at the age of eighteen to spend time working in a service-based job such as retail or food service. They say it's to give everyone a better sense of public duty and appreciation for the working class, but as Patrick and my parents have put it, it's also cheap labor since wages are subsidized through the government.

Due to my status as a Pig Farm Heiress and having access to some highly skilled family lawyers, I got out of mine. I guess it was ultimately decided that I would be 'working' for the better part of my life, even if I was only meant to be some ornamental figurehead attached to a man's arm.

They even got creative and somehow managed to get Milo out of the RIS as well. They said his job could be considered customer-facing, even though it was really just escorting me everywhere I go and making it feel like I am no different than a bookstore or coffee shop.

The store's windows are illuminated with bright colored pieces of glass as we approach and the door chimes softly when we enter and see Flame's iconic red hair pop up from behind a back counter.

"Bluebell!" she squeals, running over and throwing her arms around my neck. "You wouldn't believe the shipment we got today! Come take a look!"

I let her lead me toward the back of the shop while Milo drifted to the food service section of the store and proceeded to order something for us to share. He doesn't have to ask what I want, he just always seems to know.

The recently set sun still sends whispers of blue daylight through the window quilt of colors, but Flame has already turned on many of the solar-powered lights lining the shop's ceiling. This results in the wooden crates she's stacked by the wall looking even dirtier and dustier than The Dusting itself.

This doesn't seem to bother her though, as she rips off the lid from the nearest box and digs through its contents until she's secured a thin paperback book that she shoves into my hands.

"This!" she cries triumphantly. "This is why I wanted to work here."

"What is this..." I murmur, flipping through the pages until my fingers land on something highly, and I mean highly, inappropriate. "Whoa, are these romance novels?"

"A whole box of them!" Flame says, pretending to swoon dramatically into my arms and she's lucky I'm able to catch her before she hits the ground.

"Where are they from?" I place the book back down, my eyes lingering on the shirtless man on the cover. Flame reaches over and runs a finger gently down the glossy image, her face a dreamy mask of delight.

"That big rusty land train that stopped by here a few days ago. The same one that dropped off all that furniture by Larson's. Well, apparently, these are from the same abandoned warehouse. Can you imagine? Who would leave behind treasures like this?"

The giant land trains are beasts of machinery that travel the great stretches of nothingness between the cities and towns on this side of the country. I've never been inside one, but Hildy used to take Milo and me to the nearest docking station to watch their arrivals. They brought the thrill of travel and adventure with them and were an endless source of fascination for us. That is until we both grew up and realized that neither of us would ever be leaving Pioneer Springs.

I pick up another book and examine the cover which depicts a vast field of wheat with two lovers tangled together in its core. I put it back down quickly and hope Flame doesn't notice how red my face becomes. I've only ever kissed one boy in my life and don't have any experience with romance or anything of the sort. It's hard to get around to something like that when you're never alone and most of the city views you as some sort of prize pig that's too valuable to look at, let alone touch.

"I guess most people think books aren't as practical as medicine, food, and clothing," I say and Flame visibly pouts.

"They should be, they play a vital role in self-care."

"Bluebell, get over here and eat something before you say something offensive," Milo calls to me from across the store.

Flame giggles and nudges me hard in the ribs. I notice she's wearing the skirt I had made last week. It took me ages to have covers of her favorite books converted into fabric, but the resulting design was worth every second of labor and it spins and twirls around her ankles as if she were a moving bookcase from a fairy tale. She notices my staring and runs her hands over the shining fabric.

"I've had so many compliments on this! You have such a gift! You really should make more of them. I bet you could sell them by the bucket load."

"Are you kidding? My parents would never allow it, they indulge me enough as is. Pretty fabrics are no match for... pigs and chickens."

Flame makes a face but changes the subject quickly. "Do you want a few books to take home with you? Maybe have Milo read you a bedtime story?"

"Ew, um, no." Then I pause and reconsider. "Well...I guess I'll take one. Or two. Oh, and a magazine!"

She laughs loudly and slips a few of the smaller novels and fresh, crisp fashion magazines into a slim canvas bag and presses it into my arms with a wink that is entirely too bold.

I leave her to her crates of forgotten stories and make my way to Milo, who has taken a table by the window. He's typing something into his pager and I guess he's probably letting his fiancée know he'll be late tonight.

I know him well enough to know not to ask why he's frowning at whatever she's messaged him back. The sour look on his face is all I need to see. So, instead, I spear small pieces of fired tofu and peppers onto a fork and eat in silence until he's ready to say something. It's only after he's remained quiet for several more minutes that I finally set my fork down and kick him lightly under the table.

"Hey," I whisper and he looks up at me after slipping the pager back into his pocket.

"Hey," he whispers back and meets my stare. "You ready to head back home?"

"Truthfully? No. If I were writing my story right now, I'd stay here. I'd work this night shift with Flame and we'd read and categorize books long into the night and then eat all the ice cream from the employee fridge before closing up shop. But..."

"But..." he repeats, his usual grin reappearing on his face.

"But I don't think I have the energy to face down with Patrick again, so I guess we're headed back."

Milo sighs, opening his mouth to say something but is interrupted by the insistent buzzing from his pager, which he looks at again with a scowl before tucking it deep into his pocket once more.

"Let's go," he says gruffly, pushing away from the table and striding to the door. I turn and wave at Flame, who waves back with several more books in her hands and tells me to come back soon.

It's well into the evening as Milo and I make our way back along the same sidewalks and while the street lamps still shine, a thin layer of smoky air has settled upon the ground. It makes everything hazy and yellow. The beautiful twilight from earlier is long gone as we make our way home.

We come to the chicken manor and see that the windows and doors are all open and music streams loudly from them into the grainy night. Milo quickens his pace, his steps urgent and quick behind me and he doesn't need to tell me to walk quickly. I already know I don't want to be caught out here, not when Robbie has been having way too much fun with his so-called friends all evening.

But we aren't so lucky.

A loud and bellowing voice echoes from the mansion's open windows and to the laughter and shouts of what sounds like a horde of drunken men, Robbie Lester comes stumbling from his front door. He has trouble putting one foot in front of the other but makes it as far as the sidewalk and lurches directly into our path once more. This time though, he steps between Milo and myself so that I am cut off and staring directly into his brown and vacant expression.

"Back from your night on the town?" he asks, his words slurring together. I can see Milo try to move out from behind him, but Robbie notices him and reaches out with a thick arm to grab me around the waist.

"Master. Shaw, don't be so protective. It's not like she's *your* prize pig." He laughs, pressing his foul-smelling mouth to the side of my neck and depositing another sloppy kiss on my skin. It nearly makes me gag, but I hold my ground and grind my teeth to keep from saying anything. We've done this dance before and it should be over soon if I remain still and calm and definitely do not say what I'm really thinking.

Robbie Lester wouldn't dare hurt me or my honor, there is too much riding on our eventual union, but that doesn't mean he can't be annoyingly crass and gross.

But Milo seems not willing to play this game tonight and makes his move. I realized soon after leaving the bookshop when he refused to check the pager that I could clearly hear buzzing over and over again in his pocket, that he seemed just a little too quiet and highly strung. As if something, like Robbie getting in his way, could really set him off.

I watch now as he reaches over and yanks his arm away and spins me to his side, grabbing my wrist almost painfully. I look up and see his eyes are cold as they scan over the lumbering form before us.

"My job is to be protective of this one, lest anyone shames her honor or the honor of her family," he growls at Robbie.

"It's okay, Milo," I say, peeling his hand away and looking up at Robbie. I force a painful smile on my face. "Please don't drink too much, we're expected at brunch early tomorrow morning, remember?"

He belches loudly and nods, straightening up before Milo and glaring at him.

We've attracted an audience and several of Robbie's friends have ventured away from the manor and congregated on the lawn before us. Most of them are small in comparison, only Milo and Robbie are matched in size, and I recognize many of their faces. They wouldn't dare touch or say anything to Milo or me for fear of their jobs and reputations in this city, but Robbie laughs in Milo's face. I don't think anything scares him.

"Enjoy having this job while you can, Master Shaw. As I'm sure you're aware, your services won't be needed after the wedding," he says, puffing his chest and smiling. "After that, she'll be a Lester and I'll be the only protection she needs."

Milo's grip tightens when he tugs me down the sidewalk. We flee from the raucous sounds of laughter from Robbie's friends, and neither of us says a word until we've crossed into our estate's threshold and are well hidden among the tall and unmoving stone trees.

I sit down numbly on a bench and bend into myself, wrapping my arms around my legs and burying my head into my arms. I was never much of a crier, even when I was young. I always tried to tough it out and be brave and fearless. But that inner strength leaks out more and more as my wedding grows closer with each day. I'm afraid of what will be left of me when it finally arrives.

"I can't stand that guy," breathes Milo, taking a moment to compose himself and standing with his back turned to me. I can't see his face, but I know he's upset by Robbie's words.

"Well, like he said, you won't have to deal with the cad much longer."

"Yes, but you'll have to. You'll have to every day of your life, and I... well, it just doesn't seem right." Milo finally turns around and looks at me. I can hear his pager buzzing again in his pocket and when he notices my glance, he finally takes it out and lets loose a stream of swear words that could rival some of my own. "We should get back, I'm, um, needed at home."

"What's going on now?" I ask stiffly, lifting myself from the bench and walking shoulder to shoulder with him into our now quiet and dimly lit estate house.

"Looks like Tasha's parents have brought over more gifts," he says through gritted teeth.

"More?" I laugh. "They must really want you in the family."

"Well, of course they do. It's all about ties and connections, and since they didn't have a son to marry you and Patrick is way out of their league, they went for the next best thing and are having their only daughter marry me. Just taking a back door into the pig empire."

"They do know you won't be my guard after the... marriage?" I ask. I'm unable to keep the slight waver from my voice, but I don't think Milo notices as he opens the door to my room for me.

"I don't know," he says quietly. "I have to get going, but I'll see you tomorrow morning and will tell you all about it."

"Promise?"

"Promised." Milo smiles, crossing his fingers over his heart. "Goodnight, Bluebell."

The loud clicking sound of my bedroom door locking securely sounds in my face as Milo closes the door and I'm left alone in my room.

Letting out a sigh that could be heard throughout the town's second-largest mansion, I drag myself from the dooryard and cross my rather expansive room until I get to my sewing corner.

With Flame's skirt complete, I have time to start a new project and I begin to sketch out ideas into one of my notebooks.

Working with fashion is one of the few privileges I've been allowed. To sew and create and make all manner of I consider to be works of art. Who knows if Robbie will be okay with this hobby? He may want me to be the perfect model of the perfect wife, but I don't think I can ever let him take this away from me. Even if I've somewhat accepted the fact that I have to marry him. I at least plan to do everything in my power not to let him take anything away from me.

This is my life, the cotton and silky fabrics and colorful threads, crystal buttons, and brooches made in the shape of every item and animal known to humankind. All of it. My heart creates and stitches and contrasts art, pure art that one can display upon their body and truly express themselves for all to see. It is the act of creating a secondary soul for one to share with the whole world.

This upcoming marriage will take away my name, it will take some of my freedom and it will even take away Milo, but I will not... no, I will never let anyone take this away from me. This is where my heart sings.

Chapter Three

I wake to the smell of bacon and it makes the pit in my stomach grow. The Florence family is hosting brunch for the Lester family today and it's just the first of many family obligations I'll be required to attend. All of them leading up to the most important of them all, the unfortunate wedding.

It takes a great deal of effort to rouse from my bed and drag my sluggish body into the shower room. I don't put much effort into my appearance. It might be vain of me to think so, but I don't think I need much to look my best. Still, I rather think the Lesters are undeserving of seeing me in top form. After all, it isn't my looks they're interested in.

I've already changed into a blue dress I know my mother will approve of and am pulling a brush slowly through my curly auburn hair, not paying too much attention to the way each ringlet falls about my shoulders. A quick knocking at my door reminds me Milo has come to escort me downstairs. The sound of it unlocking is heard before he enters my room and I see immediately that he's freshly shaven and wearing his best black suit.

"Aren't you ready yet?" He teases, striding across the room and draping himself over the nearest chair. He looks like a model from a fashion magazine and I have to hide my blush.

"It takes time to look fifty percent of my best self," I inform him and he laughs loudly before remembering himself and casting me a long look.

"You don't want to get off on the front foot with the Lesters. Look at my family. One broken engagement and the Shaws couldn't mean more than chicken scat to them."

"That wasn't your fault," I say, flicking my hand in the air. "That happened before we were even born and I don't understand how anyone could hold the actions of someone's great-grandparents against them. It's incredibly stupid to hold a feud for so long."

"Well, you'd be incredibly stupid to mention anything about that feud at brunch, so I'd recommend keeping your opinions to yourself, at least for today," says Milo. He stands and holds out his arm for me to take because he's always the gentleman. "Come on, you're late enough as it is."

I put the brush down and look at myself in the mirror one more time. Half of my perfect ringlets of brown locks have flickered apart and left a halo of frizzy hair about my shoulders. I've purposely neglected to brush my teeth, hoping for my morning breath to not only stun but amaze, and I've only plastered on the barest hint of blush and eyeshadow. I do make sure I have the engagement ring on my finger, though.

I look normal, which is not what I am, but what I wish I was.

Taking Milo's elbow, I follow him out the door and walk to the first of many forced and awkward social interactions with the Lesters.

Milo is quiet as we pass through the halls and even though I give him a minute to speak, I finally break the silence when he remains quiet too long for my liking.

"So how did last night go? Did you get all of Tasha's gifts? What were they?"

He laughs stiffly and shuffles his feet as we come across the grand staircase. I can hear the murmur of voices below us and know we won't be alone much longer.

"Her parents brought her grandmother's engagement ring. It's very stylish, you'd like it. It's got a retro feel with a big green gem in the center. I don't know what kind, but you would know. They want me to use it at the ceremony."

"I see," I whisper. "What a lucky girl, it's probably much more elegant than the monstrosity on my hand."

"Well, yours is probably worth ten times as much," he whispers back and then, straightening his shoulders, he gestures grandly down the staircase. "I stopped by the kitchen before coming up. Eat the salad and bread, but skip most of the egg dishes. They were made with hog-fat. If Madam Lester is watching, eat only the deviled eggs, they won't have any meat in them and I know she'll be looking to see you sampling something chicken based."

I swallow hard and grip Milo's shoulder. "Thank you," I say softly.

"My pleasure, Miss Florence," he replies in the same soft voice and pulls me with him down the stairs. "Let's get this over with."

I'm surprised to see Mary in the dining room when Milo and I finally make our way inside. She is running circles around Hildy, who is desperately trying to chase her back out the door and into the gardens. She also has the youngest of the Lesters in tow, a boy several years her junior named George. He is the opposite of Robbie in so many ways, but mostly because he's a small and sweet child.

They graze past us and Mary giggles as she slaps a pressed wild-flower into my hand before taking off in a sprint out the door. Hildy, breathing heavily as she passes, gives me an apologetic look before heading out after her and George. I tuck the wildflower behind my ear as I watch them go, then look around the room.

My mother couldn't be any less interested in my sister's shenanigans and has positioned herself on the large, red velvet couch by the fireplace. She's a petite little thing and almost looks like she could be one of Mary's dolls. I've always been taller than her having inherited my abnormal height from my father.

Beside her sits Mrs. Patricia Lester, Robbie's stepmother and current matriarch of the Lester household. I can't hear what they're talking about, but I have no doubt that it deals with the running of each of their empires. Yet no matter how much power and sway these two women may hold between them, they both succumb to the will of their even more powerful husbands. That has been the way around here for as long as I can remember.

Mr. Roland Lester, Robbie's large and intimidating father, stands off to the side with Patrick and Robbie. Their faces are flushed as if they might have recently finished a round of drinks and they are leaning together eagerly discussing something of what I suppose they consider great importance. I find I rather don't care to think about what that could be.

Milo's father, Mr. Martin Shaw, has posted himself by the window and has his head bent closely to my father as they too discuss something seemingly important.

The sudden movement of three different groups looking up at my entrance from their isolated conversations is unnerving and my first instinct is to bolt back through the door. But Milo is there, standing in my way and I have no choice but to venture forward and primly take Roland Lester's outstretched hand.

He kisses the top of my wrist with just as sloppy a gesture as his son before brazenly looking over my body.

"How kind of you to join us, my dear," he says in his deep and bold voice. He doesn't even acknowledge Milo when he moves to stand by my side.

"Oh yes, now that our guest of honor has risen," says my mother as she stands and floats towards us with an iron look in her eyes. "We can finally begin our brunch."

Robbie's mother claps excitedly and clasps her small hands around Robbie's formidable bicep. In this moment, I can really see how much younger she is compared to my mother, and to even Mr. Lester himself, but her smile is at least genuine as she looks at me. I turn to ask Milo if he knows how old she is, but he's already abandoned me to speak with his father by the window.

"We had our kitchen staff bring over some of our family's favorite delicacies for today," Patricia Lester says kindly, letting go of her son and pulling me towards her.

"Oh..." I stammer. "That was very kind of you."

Robbie lets out a throaty laugh directed at me.

"If she'll even eat it. Rumor has it that this one only eats sticks and grass," he says to Patrick's nervous chuckle.

"I'm sure my sister would be delighted to share in your bounty," Patrick cuts in and places a hand on my shoulder, his fingers
digging into my skin as he directs me to the table. "Isn't that right,
Bluebell?"

I stand firmly, making him stumble when I don't move.

"I am only on the minor side of hunger today, but I'll sample
what I can," I say, smiling sweetly at Mrs. Lester and escorting
myself to the table without the aid of my brother.

Milo is back by my side in an instant and pulling a chair out
for me as I take my position at the table across from Robbie, who
looks bored as he rolls a butter knife between his fingers. Patrick
sits next to him and at the head of the table sits my father with the
far opposite end reserved for my mother.

"My dear Patricia," my father says kindly, passing Robbie's
mother a basket of hot and flaky bread. "You are looking lovely
today, this weather must be as kind to you as it is to our stocks."

"Oh yes, indeed!" Patricia Lester squeals. "I haven't felt this
young in years." She gives a girlish laugh and I wonder what she
even means, the girl can't be any older than I am. "In fact, I was
just telling Tilda how I took the ladies down to the station last
night after supper. You wouldn't believe what we saw! An hon-
est-to-goodness circus train! A real beast of a land train at that!"

Robbie lets out a huff of air before stabbing a glistening sausage
with his knife. "Probably picking up more kids for the Required
Service. As if it isn't bad enough already that our factory labor has
to compete with local retail, I bet we'll lose even more to those
freaks."

"Precisely!" Robbie's father spits before continuing to shovel large quantities of bread pudding into his mouth. "The circus, bah!"

"Bluebell, sweetie, you must try the egg bites. They are quite exquisite," my mother insists, gesturing for the nearest server to bring them directly to me. Then, with my mother's scowl and urgent waving of her hands, the same server deposits one directly in the middle of my plate.

I feel Milo tense beside me and I don't have to ask why because I can see the studs of bacon gleaming with freshly fried pig fat. The entire table has turned their eyes to me with Patrick's the most intense of all, and it's to my utter horror and absolute shock that I use my knife to cut a small corner off the wobbling disc and use the smallest fork at my disposal to place it in my mouth. Refusing to look at anyone, I keep my eyes trained on the little cloud logos sprinkled along the edge of my plate.

I barely chew because I want to swallow and get it over with as quickly as possible, but as soon as I do and take a deep breath afterward, I can feel the collective sigh of relief from each of my family members, even from Milo.

"She's human after all," Robbie says, his lips curling into a satisfied smirk as he raises a glass of beer to his lips.

"Eating another living thing doesn't define your humanity," I spit back and am about to stay more when a darkness flashes across his face warning me to hold my tongue. I think he laughs lowly under his breath but doesn't look too happy.

The stares around me along with the idle chatter and the total indifference to anything outside the world of meat eating and meat processing makes bile rise to the back of my throat and I find myself rising to my feet. My palms are sweaty as I push away from the table and stand as gracefully as my shaking form will allow before excusing myself from the room by making some lame excuse of needing to use the restroom.

The conversation continues without me as I hurry to the door, my shoulder nearly smacking an incoming server before I find myself alone in the hallway with my breaths coming in quickly and angrily.

I fight the urge to vomit the food I just consumed because if I'm going to be forced to eat meat, I will at least honor the little soul that provided it for me. I'm so focused on holding my stomach and willing the food to stay in place that I don't notice the figure walking up to me until it's too late.

I look up expecting to see Milo's concerned face but instead, I find myself face to face with Robbie Lester. And he is smiling something awful.

"Tasty, wasn't it?" he asks, leaning casually against the wall beside me. "My grandmother's recipe."

"It was fine," I lie. I straighten up beside him and back up a few paces because he's so close that I can feel his hot breath on me.

He matches my steps and comes closer anyway.

"My father was a bit perturbed to see the Shaws were afforded an invite today, I doubt he'll be so willing to compromise next time. Though it's about time you rid yourself of your little bodyguard, I can send someone from my detail to... keep an eye on you."

"We have a contract." The words have trouble making their way through my clenched jaw. "There's no need."

"You're such an idiot," Robbie muses, turning towards the wall. Without warning, he slams his hands against it, his palms barely missing both my ears as he presses closer until his face is aligned with my own. I let out a small gasp that no one was around to hear.

"Idiot girls make the best wives, they're easier to train," he continues. "But your problem is that your parents let you run around like an untrained dog and without a master to guide you, you've become way too independent. Once everything is official, you'll be answering to me and I'll make sure you're groomed into the obedient wife you were born to be. And I'm sure you know all about the needs that will be required of you soon enough, little sugar plum."

I try to wiggle out from under his arms, but with one hand, he catches both of mine and grips it tightly. His free hand traces a line down my cheek and my head swivels around looking for Milo or anyone else who could be close by, but we're alone in the empty hall. The hair on my arms stands on end as I turn my gaze up and find his leering eyes cold and slimy like the big toads I used to catch with Milo when we were children.

"See? Isn't being alone with me a delicious feeling?" he says lowly, bending in close and inhaling the air by my neck.

"About as delicious as a pig fart."

He pushes my shoulders roughly away and my back slams against the wall with a sickening thud. It sends a jolt of pain up my spine and tears spring into my eyes. Is this what my life is going to be like once we're boned for life? I knew Robbie wore a cold mask, but I didn't realize it hid such a dirty and dark heart. How am I supposed to marry someone like this?

"I'm not sure what you're expecting from this union, but I can tell you this now. You will not be permitted to speak this way to me when we're married," he growls at me as the sounds of a nearby door swinging open falls upon me like a glorious ray of sunshine.

"Master Lester," Milo's soothing voice carries over to us and brings Robbie's attention to the door. "Your parents require you."

Robbie doesn't even spare me a glance as he straightens his suit jacket and brushes past me. Milo steps effortlessly out of his way, his eyes trained on the ground and then closes the door securely behind him after he leaves.

"Are you okay?" he asks softly. He comes over and places a hand on my shoulder and even though the touch is as light as a feather, the emotions of my interaction with Robbie weigh me to the floor like a ton of bricks. I slide down and sit there, staring at nothing ahead of me until Milo clears his throat and squats beside me.

I turn to him, not even caring about the tears streaming down my face. A nearby window has been left open and it carries in the fragrance of flowers and freshly polished stone trees, and the light... the light is beautiful and pale and silky yellow like fresh butter. It's a moment full of life and promise, but it also helps settle something in me. A thought that I haven't yet allowed myself to consider.

Robbie Lester can bury himself in a pile of moldy chicken scat.

"I can't do it," I whisper to Milo, to myself, to the hallway and to my small world. "I can't marry him."

Chapter Four

Y esterday I had Milo lock me in my room and instructed him to return to brunch and make up some excuse as to why I couldn't come back. I'm beyond caring what any of them think so I stayed in there the rest of the day.

Today though, is Milo's day off and I only remember it when I wake to the solid and formidable knocking of someone else. Their sharp knuckles rap impatiently on my door so just to spite them, I take my time coming to open it. Usually, a man named Warren takes over when Milo is away and for all intents and purposes, he's a good bodyguard, but he's very, very boring. He's also much more intimidating than Milo and carries around an assortment of weapons on his belt, including a nasty metal wire I know he can use to choke people. I hear he used to work for the Lesters and that many of them carry such 'protection.'

Trying not to think about how I wish Milo was here today, I get myself dressed as quickly as possible because I don't want any unplanned social obligations being sprung on me last minute. I would trust Milo to head them off before they got past the door to my room, but I don't trust Warren with that kind of privacy.

I find an old, pink jumpsuit I once constructed out of a discarded bed sheet and pull it on. The buttery fabric feels soft and airy against my skin and I think it must be the perfect thing to wear on a warm spring day. A pair of dirty sneakers complete the look, even though I know they'll earn me a stern lecture from my mother if she catches me wearing them. I remember the engagement ring and slip it on my finger, so at least she won't be able to complain about that if she sees me.

Warren steps aside as I leave my room and I only catch him once glancing at my dirty shoes before I begin briskly walking down the hall ahead of him. I know I can't really outrun the guy. I tried once before, but I've learned to keep just the right pace to keep him far enough so I can at least pretend he's not there.

I don't tell him where we're going, but I'm assuming he can guess as there is really only one place I go to in town. Well, maybe one of two, but Sparrow's Books, Coffee, and Tea is the most common. It's also a place that I know Warren will stay out of because, unlike Milo, he prefers outside on a bench. I don't think he's ever come inside the shop before, I don't even know if he likes coffee... or if he knows how to read.

"Bluebell!" Flame shrieks from behind the counter as I dart inside, letting the door close in Warren's face.

"Flame!" I yell back at her. I cross the empty store and perch on an empty chair beside the shop's food counter.

She grins and begins preparing a drink for me, a tall frothy concoction of coffee, oat milk and cinnamon. It's been my favorite for a very long time, ever since I weaned myself off vanilla lattes. I've never paid for one with our family's estate having an ongoing tab set up for me, and Flame always just pushes a few buttons on her console to settle my bill.

And that's how it's always happened, except today it doesn't work. Flame makes a face at the screen and pushes several more buttons and frowns deeply before pushing the drink in my direction and looking at me.

"The payment was declined," she says, almost as if she can't believe she's even having to say those words to me. My eyes grow wide as she spins the screen in my direction so that I can see the big and dramatic PAYMENT DENIED pulsing in my face.

I slam my palms on the table, redness creeping up my neck and bruising my face. Flame just looks sad as she pushes the drink even closer.

"Take the drink, I already made it. Maybe it's a mistake?"

"I don't think so," I tell her, sliding my hands off the counter and turning away from the flashing words. "It was probably Patrick, or maybe my parents freezing my accounts. Yesterday's brunch didn't go very well."

"Does it matter? You're already tied to that brute. An awkward waffle or two can't make that much of a difference."

"It can make enough of one." I sigh. I turn towards the window to see Warren has positioned himself on a nearby bench and is bent deep into a small tablet he holds in his hands. Maybe he knows how to read after all.

Still, as a precaution, I gesture for Flame to follow me towards the back of the store. She nods and points to a small table in the corner and wipes down the counter a few times before meeting me there. Her green eyes scan me over before she says anything. "What happened?"

"Robbie Lester is a slimy toad," I start. "He cornered me and told me what he expects of me as his wife, which I can only assume is the equivalent to a breeding sow." I can't help the shudder that travels up my body and Flame reaches out to hold both my hands in her own.

"You knew things were going to change," she says with slow and measured words. "Still, we both thought it wouldn't be that bad."

"The closer we get to that wedding date, the more I feel like my life is slipping away. I thought I was okay with not getting what I wanted from life, but he expects...You know, I talked back to him and he told me I couldn't do that again or there would be consequences." Tears start to well in my eyes and Flame hands me a clean napkin. "I know I should be scared of him, but I think I'm just angry. Angry at him, at my life, and at this stupid, stupid marriage."

"And I know it's not the only arranged marriage you're angry at," Flame says kindly, reaching back and squeezing my hands. Her comments make the tears come hard and I squeeze my eyes shut and will they to stop.

"Milo is the least of my concerns," I say through gritted teeth. "I need to take care of myself first."

Flame nods along with my comments, though I don't think she believes my comment regarding Milo. She sits back in her chair with a thoughtful look. "Let's look at the big-ticket items here, you live with a family who doesn't appreciate you and you're engaged to some idiot who thinks you're on the same level as breeding stock. Have you thought about leaving?"

"Leaving? Like leaving Pioneer Springs?"

Flame nods.

"I, uh, I don't even know where I would go. I've never been anywhere outside of town." I start to clean up my face with the napkin.

"To be fair, there is only one way to go." Flame points out, gesturing with a hand towards the eastern haze of the Dusting. "And not to offend, but you don't seem like the roughing it type to try crossing that."

Flame has always had a fascination with our vast and unknown backyard, and I have sort of always known she would one day pack up her books and jump the first land train set on crossing those dead and wild lands. I don't think the Western dream has ever interested her, but the stories and pictures of sparkling oceanside parties I see in every fashion magazine have always tempted me.

"But how would I even get there?" I whisper and Flame shrugs. "That's something we'll have to figure out quickly, but I guess you could always hitch a ride with the circus."

"The circus?"

"Yup, they're in town recruiting for the Required Service, you could get an interview, go with them to the next town and then disappear. You could probably sell that chunk of a rock on your finger and you'd be set for some time. I'm sure they'd take you in a heartbeat and then you could just disappear before anyone figures out where you are. It's kind of romantic when you think about it."

I laugh, the tears on my face now dry. "I think you've been reading too much."

"There is no such thing and you know it," she says with a smile. "But since you can't pay for anything and you owe me for that drink, why don't you help me sort some books. Remember those crates we just got? Well, the best stuff was way at the bottom. And I do mean..."

We're interrupted by the shop's door swinging open and the little bell on the hinges ringing wildly to let us know we're no longer alone. Flame points to the crate and stands to help the new customers, but I find I can't even look at the dirty boxes in the corner because I'm too intrigued by the small group of people who have just entered the store. I lean from my chair to get a better look at them and can't help but let out a small gasp.

They look like they're from the circus.

The two people that entered the shop couldn't look any different. One is short and round and has a soft look to his face despite his very loud choice of clothing and bright green, spiky hair. He's wearing what I think is a red velvet robe with a logo from the Cloudspeak Company stitched upon the breast and has at least ten different piercings in each ear.

His companion is a tall girl about my age. She has long, blond hair that falls in soft waves along her shoulders and her eyes are big and blue as she takes in the stacks of books around the shop. She wears a simple green dress that is entirely too pretty, but there is a mischievous look in her eyes that tells me she would make a fun friend.

"Welcome!" Flame's friendly voice rings out and the girl barely spares her a glance as she zeros in on the stacks of romance novels by the wall. She gives a high-pitched squeal as she rushes to them, sliding on her knees so that she can closely inspect each and every title along their paperback spines. Flame, true to her nature, doesn't take any offense to the slight and merely nods her approval over the girl's taste in books as she walks over to help.

The short man, however, snaps his fingers at me and declares in a high and dramatic voice, "What does one have to do to get a drink around here?"

"What kind are you looking for?" I ask, edging close to the pile of romance novels. I'd rather take my chances there than attempt to make this man a drink.

"The dirty kind." He laughs, throwing a silky scarf over his shoulder. "But this doesn't look like the kind of place that offers that kind of thing, so a black coffee will have to do."

I stare at him and he stares back at me and neither of us move until I realize he's expecting me to serve him. My face turns scarlet and I look to Flame for help, but she's busy showing off another crate of racy books to the tall girl.

"Oh, um, I guess I can help you with that," I stammer and he watches with interest as I make my way behind the counter and quickly wash my hands.

"Will you be drinking that here, or would you like a travel cup?" I remember to ask. Luckily I've ordered enough coffee drinks from Flame to somewhat know what I'm doing.

"Travel, dear, travel," he repeats, looking over his shoulder and calling to his friend. "Minty, did you want anything? I'm not asking twice."

The girl stands, clutching several books close to her chest. One nearly falls, but Flame offers her a canvas bag to store them in.

Then, without her noticing, Flame sticks a few more inside and winks at me.

"Oh, no," says Minty. "I'll have just enough for these and nothing left for fancy drinks I'm afraid."

"Priorities," says Flame with a sage nod. "I like you."

The girl presses some money into Flame's hands and I can see from here that it's a collection of crumpled and wadded single bills. The man at the counter notices as well and shakes his head at her. The singles he passes over have at least been pressed and cleanly smoothed out.

I pour him a large cup of coffee in the same kind of travel cups I've seen Flame give me and while I'm impressed at my work, what little of it I did, I'm still glad when Flame comes over and takes care of his payment.

"Are you from the new land train?" she asks him, counting some change that she hands over to him.

"We are!" Minty says brightly. "Snuzzle rarely gets off the train, but I convinced him to come with me so that I can see what a town this close to the Dusting is like. It's, um, nice."

Flame and I laugh.

"It can be," I say. "But when the wind blows just right, it can be a living nightmare."

"I guess I could see that," Minty says, clutching her bag of books closely. "But it's the towns out here, this close to the border, that always have the best stuff. You know, with everything collected from... out there."

"We are known for that. Well, that and also pigs and chickens. Plenty of those around here," I say and Snuzzle wrinkles his nose at me.

"Yes, I gathered that just as soon as I stumbled off the train."

"Oh, it sounds like such a romantic life," Flame gushes. "Freedom to roam the wilds, performances by the glittering seaside cities, new towns, new cities..."

Minty nods enthusiastically. "If it's something you're interested in, they holding interviews for a few Required Service positions."

"Is it hard to get selected?" I ask and Minty shrugs.

"I don't think so, they let me join!"

"That reminds me," says Snuzzle. He pulls out a rolled-up notice from a long pocket in his robe and hands it to Flame. As she unrolls it, I give his outfit a long look.

"I like the boldness of your outfit," I tell him. My hand automatically comes out and taps at the logo patch. "But this looks like it could do with a few touchups. The threads are starting to unravel on the sides."

He runs his hand over the patch fondly before eyeing me, his fingers lingering on the sparkling stones of my ring.

"And I like the boldness of your attitude, what did you say your name was?"

"Oh," I stutter. Sometimes I forget that not everyone knows the Florence family. "Bluebell, Bluebell Florence."

"Oh, are you related to the pig dealers?" Minty asks. "I overheard someone saying we were getting a shipment of bacon on the train, something about a Florence family specialty."

"Yup, that's her, the princess of Swiney Acres," Flame points out and Minty giggles.

"Well, your highness," says Snuzzle. "Since this is your kingdom, maybe you can help us. Now that this one has completed her errand, I'm hoping to run one of my own and get a little shopping done. Do you know of the best place to buy things you may not want, but someone else needs?"

Flame looks thoughtful at his comment, but I can't help the grin that spreads across my face. My frustrations at my own family, as well as the Lesters and Shaws, feel distant as I gesture towards the door.

"Come with me, I know just the place."

Chapter Five

Warren raises an eyebrow when I exit the store with Minty and Snuzzle, but I avoid making any sort of eye contact with him as we make our way down the street toward one of the best shops in town.

The sky above is crystal blue, but as Minty and Snuzzle comment on its beauty, I have to tell them that such skies are usually bad omens around here and we're due for a bad storm any day now.

Snuzzle matches my brisk stride and peppers me with questions about the history of Pioneer Springs. I tell him what I can remember from history lessons in school, which isn't a lot, so I quickly run out of answers. Minty follows behind us at a slower pace and I realize she walks with a terrible limp. I practically bite my tongue from holding back asking her, or Snuzzle, where it came from, but I can hear Milo in my head right now telling me to keep quiet about it and that it would be considered rude.

Luckily, we made it to Theo's Threadshop and Gifts before Snuzzle could question me about all the old solar cars lined up along the street. While I do know a lot about them thanks to Patrick and Milo telling me all about them, they also stir up some older memories I've tried my very best to bury deep inside my mind. I take great care to avoid walking by or even looking at, the deep red one on the corner. That car belongs to Milo.

"This is the place!" I tell them, stopping to hold the door open for both of them to enter the building.

Snuzzle whistles in amusement as we walk inside and Minty gasps in delight, and it's all I need to know I've chosen the right place to take them. Theo's is my favorite store and for a very good reason.

Because Pioneer Springs borders so close to the Dusting and is a great stopping point for many people, we have the first choice of all the treasures left behind. Those who dare venture into the inhospitable lands often return with even rarer and more unusual things and the stuff that isn't sold to anyone in town is picked up by the land trains passing through. I suppose our city could be considered the biggest second-hand store in the whole country.

While there are a few cities devoted to producing new items like clothing and furniture and the like, the market for barely used items has made a good living for a large number of people. It's something that's always fascinating Flame, though I think she'd drive head-on into that big cloud of dust if it meant she could get her hands on a few rare and out of print books. That's just the kind of person she is.

"This is really something!" Minty says with a stunned expression on her face. "We have big rooms and lots of things on the train, but I've never seen so much... stuff!"

I chuckle and watch as Snuzzle brushes past us with a wave over his shoulder and makes a straight line to the rows upon rows of colorful clothing.

"This is one of my favorite places. This town may drive me crazy, but I like knowing I can come here and lose myself in a place like this. Like the lives that everything here once led were here to give me a little of their light."

"That sounds dreamy." Minty sighs. "If the town drives you nuts, you could always apply with us. Magenta is always looking for a new Stage girl to replace the ones we keep losing."

"Who is Magenta and what's a Stage Girl? Also, why would you keep losing them?"

Minty laughs and her blonde curls bounce around her shoulders.

"Well, we don't actually lose them, they just move on. Oh dear, that sounds worse, what I mean is that they just disappear into the night... no, wait..."

"What she means to say is that most of them, and it's not just the girls, sign up just for their Required Service credit and a free ride out of town," says a nearby girl with long coppery hair.

Minty looks away with a deep blush on her cheeks and I turn to the newcomer with a sour look.

"I gathered that, but who is Magenta and what do the Stage Girls do?"

"She's our boss," Minty says softly, avoiding looking at the new girl who has since moved away, and leaning close to me. "That's Rose, she gets off at every single stop and is on the hunt, if you know what I mean."

When I shake my head, Minty pulls me closer and whispers in my ear, "She's looking for a husband. Her Required Service is up, but rumor has it that she hasn't saved enough to leave the train yet so she's looking for someone to pay the bills. The Stage Girls do absolutely everything, in my opinion, and we get a lot of tips on top of the work we do, which as I said, is everything. We help cook, serve guests, run the shows, sometimes perform in the shows, and anything else you can imagine goes into running a big-time circus."

"Hmm." I hum, thinking about the idea. "It sounds like a lot of work."

I don't admit it to her, but I've never actually held a real job. Sure, I've helped Flame out occasionally in the shop, but no one outside my family has held a position of power over me and directed me to 'work' for them. And what she's currently describing to me sounds like something that requires a lot of effort.

"It is a lot of work," she admits. "But it's not so bad when you do it with people you like, but I guess that can be said about any job. Though it's a surefire way to change things up and get out of town."

"Is that why you joined up with them?" I blurt out. This time, my cheeks go red. I know I sometimes say things before thinking them through, but I don't want to offend this girl, she seems so nice.

"We all have something we're running from," Minty replies, not at all embarrassed. "Mine was pretty straightforward. I had too many brothers and sisters and my parents couldn't afford all of us. When Magenta's Magical World of Circus Curiosities came around, I couldn't afford a ticket so I snuck under a fence and watched them warming up before their performance. It was pure magic! They had open interviews for the RIS afterward and I applied right away and left the very next morning."

"Did your family try to stop you?" I ask.

"No, why would they?" I detect the slightest tinge of sadness in her words, but she covers it with a bright smile. "It worked out for everyone in the end."

"Girls!" Snuzzle's voice rings out through the store and more than a few people turn to look. "Girls, come here, I need your opinions!"

"Anyway, think about it. If you're looking for a way out of... well, anything. This is a good way to do it," Minty tells me quickly before hurrying to find Snuzzle amongst the racks of clothing.

I follow behind her with all kinds of thoughts buzzing in my head like flies on the back of a hog.

Could I do it? Could I simply run away and join the circus? I think I could, but even if every part of me aches to go, something... someone, holds me back. Because as much as I don't want to admit it to anyone, let alone myself, I couldn't leave without Milo.

Then, as if I conjured him myself, the door behind me opens and the man himself walks inside the store. His face is set in grim, hard lines as Warren steps up behind him with matching concern. The two of them immediately begin to scan the store for me and I do the only thing I can think of in the moment. I quickly disappear into the endless field of clothing in search of my new friends.

If Milo is looking for me on his day off and Warren has set foot inside a store without me dragging him by the arm, then something's wrong and I'd rather not deal with it right now. But to be fair, there are a lot of things I'd rather not deal with at the moment.

"Whoa, look at this!" I hear Minty yelp and it helps me to find both her and Snuzzle standing next to a circular rack of grey-colored clothing. She's holding something up and looks very proud of herself. Snuzzle rolls his eyes at her and waves her off as he moves to the next rack that holds much brighter colors.

"I think it's pretty," I tell her, admiring the coloring of the dress she holds. It's so pale grey it could almost be considered blue. "Like the sky in the early morning or a pale river stone."

"You're so poetic, you should be a writer," Minty says, shoving the dress deep into the overflowing basket by Snuzzle's feet.

"No, I hear they make terrible money. I'd rather be the main character of my own story."

"Oh? What kind of story?" Minty asks with excitement written across her features.

"The kind that takes the heroine far, far away from home and where..."

But I don't get to finish my thought because Warren is suddenly there and his face is red with anger. I give him a sheepish grin and open my mouth to say something, but his rage speaks first.

"Stop hiding in here, we need to go now." He reaches out a meaty arm and grabs at my shoulder, but I duck away at the last moment.

"It's barely lunchtime," I whine in return. "I don't have to be home for hours."

"It's true, we need to head back," says Milo stepping into view. I can see Minty craning her neck to get a better look at him from behind the clothing rack she's hiding behind. Snuzzle also stands nearby, arms crossed and watching the interaction with a curious look on his face.

"But why?" I ask and Milo snuffles his feet nervously before finally looking into my eyes.

"There's been an... accident at Swiney and Warren got a call to let him know he needs to bring you back to the house right away."

I can feel the color drain from my face and become as opaque and monotone as the racks of clothing around us. The last time I was summoned home like this was when... was when...

"We should go," I say, resisting the urge to slap myself and keep the memories at bay a little while longer. I turn to Snuzzle and Minty, who have waited patiently and politely during the exchange. "I hope you enjoy the rest of your stay in Pioneer Springs," I tell them. Snuzzle raises an eyebrow at me, but Minty gives me a sad smile.

"Remember to think about it," she reminds me and I open my mouth to thank her, but Milo tugs me away at the last second and the words come out as gibberish as I'm pulled out the front doors.

If I had any color left in my complexion after hearing there was an accident, the solar car waiting to rush me back home even quicker than the five minutes it would take to walk makes my legs buckle.

Milo and Warren practically carry me and stuff me through the door and into one of the plush fabric seats. I'm hugging my knees into my chest as I hear Warren jump into the driver's seat and begin speeding down the dusty streets toward home.

"Milo?" I breathe and look over at him. He meets my eyes, but shakes his head and doesn't respond.

So that's it then. Whatever happened must be bad. Bad enough for someone with such authority to tell even Milo to keep his mouth shut and no amount of whatever is between us could stand in the way of him not doing his job.

But something isn't adding up. If whatever happened is so terrible, why are we stopping by the Lester Mansion and why has Milo's face gone from a blank and emotionless slate to a kind of screwed up pain and torture? Even Warren has slowed the car and we're no longer careening through the streets, but gliding to a slow and graceful stop in front of the Lester's grandiose front doors.

After wiping my sweaty palms on my jumpsuit, I shuffle my dirty sneakers and see Milo finally crack into a small smile when he notices them.

"Mrs. Florence is going to have some choice words about those," he muses before turning his eyes back to the window.

"I didn't care before and don't care now," I tell him as we wait in silence while Warren exits the car and approaches my door. "What is all this about?" I demand from him after having stepped out. He looms over me like an angry storm cloud and rolls his eyes towards Milo, who I see now is dressed smartly in a navy-colored suit.

"We were sent to escort you back here as quickly as possible and instructed not to say a word to you in the process," Milo tells me quietly, gesturing towards the big doors and offering me his arm to hold onto.

"Why would I be wanted here?" I ask. It's a struggle to get the words out as Milo gently leads me not to the big door, but around the expansive house's side and into the back gardens.

At some point, we lose Warren and it's just the two of us when he deposits me in front of a pretty looking tent. The silken fabric flutters in the breeze and when I look closely, I can see the imprints of a million pale pink flowers. It's the most beautiful thing I've ever seen and it serenely breaths with the fresh breeze blowing in from the west, the air sweet and untainted by dust.

"Milo?" I ask again when he remains quiet and he removes my hand, which I now realize had been digging into his arm.

"The answer is inside that tent," he tells me softly and leans in to kiss the side of my face. His lips press into the blushing skin of my cheek and he then turns as if to kiss the other side, but instead I hear his quiet whispering voice. It reminds me of how he sounded just before he kissed me last summer in the backseat of his crimson-colored solar car.

"What's in the tent?" I whisper.

"The beginning of the rest of your life," he tells me and walks away.

Chapter Six

When I enter the gorgeous tent, the first thing I see is Mary. Someone has dressed her in a flowing white dress as if it were a miniature version of a wedding gown, and that is when a horrible thought dawns upon me and my insides twist and turn and tumble around. I've walked into my own wedding.

They tricked me into coming here. Accident indeed! The anger boils under my skin and even though I'm sure both Milo and Warren had no choice in the matter, the thought that someone, most likely Patrick, thought this was the best way to seal my fate is a kind of burning torture. For a moment, I consider standing my ground, but the thoughts and fears and doubts and all other kinds of nonsense that run through my head makes me pause a moment too long.

Before I can turn and bolt from my predetermined destiny, my mother is there and her hand is iron around my wrists. It is a shackle and even though I scream at her to let go, she hisses through her teeth for me to stop. "Will you be quiet, you're embarrassing me," she snarls, throwing my arm down to my side with so much force I feel a pop in my shoulder blade. I rub my arm and glare at her.

"What is all this?" I ask and she peers up at me between her lashes. She is wearing a lot of makeup on her face and the pale skin I know I share with her is hidden behind a barrier of rose tinted plaster.

Today's lip color of choice is a deep, candy red and has been flawlessly applied to make her lips appear bigger than they already are. I want to tell her it's an awful color for her skin tone, but the last time I did something like that, she slapped my face and had Warren lock me in my room for the day.

"What do you think it is?" she asks, the annoyance clear on her face and causing a wrinkle to form between the coating over her eyebrows. She grabs my hand to check for the ring and adds, "You're getting married today!"

I balk at her words, even though I think I already know the answer.

"The wedding isn't for another few weeks!" I stutter, trying again to turn around and leave, but a few of my mother's friends have moved in and surrounded me between them. One of them, Milo's own mother I think, stands behind me and pushes me forward into the center of the tent. The rest of the women swarm upon me like flies as my mother barks commands at them from a plush chair set up for her. I will have to wait until they've all left the tent before I can even attempt to get out of here.

They twist me before a mirror and I'm poked and prodded at by them as if they were hummingbirds and I'm a floppy and pathetic flower being sucked dry of all life. The only thing that brings a smile to my face is Mary as she flies about holding a melting chocolate bar in her chubby hands. Hildy is hot on her heels but no one here has been able to catch her yet.

And I hope no one ever does and that my sweet little sister stays wild and free for as long as she can.

"Hold still," warns Mrs. Shaw as she fastens a long white veil into my hair with several straight and dangerous looking pins. I heed her warning, but can't stop a few tears from sliding down the cheek her own son just kissed goodbye. She doesn't even notice.

"Tilda, you've outdone yourself with this event," one of the women coos near my ear and I can see my mother beaming at her from her throne. "It will be the talk of the city for years to come."

"Yes, it wasn't easy with everything being so last minute. And as you know, fresh floral arrangements can be such a challenge at this time of year, but I was able to make it work."

I fight the urge to roll my eyes at her remarks.

"Stunning," another one of my mother's followers admires from my other side while she fixes small blue ribbons to the side of my veil. One of them curls into my eyes and I keep having to swat it away in annoyance. Every time I open my mouth to say something to someone, one of these chickens starts talking over me. It's exasperating to have them all stand there as if I don't exist and I shift from foot to foot as I become increasingly uncomfortable with the twittering conversation and having to stand still for so long.

But no one around seems to notice my growing discomfort and the unease from knowing that this may be my life going forward begins to pool in my belly making me want to crawl into a hole and hide. To make matters worse, my stomach lets out a loud grumble in protest from not having time for lunch.

Everything happening all at once, makes it hard to think, but I know that I need to get out of here because I refuse to end up married today, even if there is cake. And I love cake.

I also love this dress and as much as my skin crawls at the thought of becoming Mrs. Robbie Lester, Queen of Chickens, I have to admit the wedding dress is an absolutely stunning piece of clothing. It looks as if it was handmade by someone, definitely not any of the chickens around me now, and cinches in perfectly at my waist with cascading fabric that circles my arms with a fluttering softness. It even has enough skirt to cover my longer legs and the shimmering fabric is such a light blue that it could be a sheet of a thousand ice crystals.

I lift my foot and rub at the fabric with my toes, my dirty sneakers long since ripped off and tossed to the side, and marvel at how smooth and luxurious it feels. I feel almost as if I was a princess in one of Mary's story books, except there is no prince charming waiting for me.

I'm about to ask someone where they found such a dress but a loud ringing bell begins to chime through the air and the women around start to scream in delight as Milo's mother pats my cheek with her hand.

"It's time! We're going to take our seats and someone will be in soon to escort you down the aisle. Oh, you look so pretty! We found this dress for Tasha, but that blue absolutely clashed with her complexion and we had to search for something much more suitable for a wedding to my dear sweet Milo. At least it looks wonderful on you!" Mrs. Shaw fusses with my hair one last time and helps me to step into a pair of plain blue heels before she hurries after the other women filing out of the tent.

My mother is nowhere to be seen as she must have been the first to leave the tent, but Mary magically appears at my side and tugs at my gown with a, thankfully, clean hand.

"You look pretty." She giggles before running away and darting through the tent flap Hildy holds open for her. She leaves me alone so quickly that I don't even have a chance to say goodbye or tell her I love her and that I'm so sorry, but I plan on leaving her behind.

The thought brings tears to my eyes again and I'm turning to look at myself one last time in the mirror before making a break for it when I hear the tent flap ripple open once again and I turn to see Milo standing at the entrance.

"Hi," he says, but I don't reply right away because the annoyance at him is building in my core and I watch as he shuffles his feet a few times before looking away. That's when I take my chance.

"How long have you known they were going to trick me?" I ask and he doesn't look up when he replies.

"Not long, just a few days."

"Wonderful." I sigh, gathering the silky skirt in my fists and kicking off the slippers. They are too tight on my feet and I struggle and hop around until I can pry both of them off. I then throw them with all my might at the tent wall, but they bounce harmlessly off and fall into the dirt.

Milo watches in silence, then walks to the opposite side of the tent to gather my sneakers, which he tosses to me one by one. "Mrs. Florence isn't going to like you wearing those shoes," he says.

"You mistake me for someone who cares," I sing back, pushing my feet easily into the familiar shoes. I then move to sit at a small table set up with a mirror and begin removing a few of the needle-like hair pins that keep making their way deeper and deeper into my skull.

Something has clicked inside me and I feel... disconnected. Soft music plays outside the tent and I can make out the murmur of soft voices. The sweet smell of cake and frosting even floats by my nose for a small moment, and when I close my eyes, I can imagine what it's like out there. It's beautiful and perfect, but it's not perfect for me.

Lost in my thoughts, I misjudged pulling one of the sharp pins out and stabbing my finger. Blood pools in a small bubble on the end of my fingertip and I press it down upon the white lace tablecloth below me. It leaves a smear of red against the pristine fabric and while I hate to dirty something so nice, the contrast of color is more beautiful than pretty dresses, tasty cakes and soft floral arrangements. It is something more. Like me.

"Milo..." I begin by choosing my words carefully and slowly.

"We need to get going," he says, still not meeting my eyes.

"You're right, we do." I stand up, gripping the dress in my sweaty palms. My feet feel much better now, enough to do what I know I need to do. To run.

"Ready, then?" he asks, holding out his arm and stepping beside the tent flap that I know leads to what he told me was the beginning of the rest of my life. I swallow hard and don't budge from the mirror.

"I'm not going," I tell him and this time he looks at me, his eyes boring into mine as he takes a step forward. He's so close I could kiss him and hug him and grab his hand and pull him with me back out the way I came.

"What are you..." he blurts out, but I throw my hand over his mouth and glare at him.

"I refuse to marry that pile of pig scat out there. I'm leaving. Now."

Milo pulls my hand away from his mouth but lowers his voice. "Look, I know you're not happy about this. It's been very obvious lately, but you know you have to go through with it right? This is what your family wants."

"Exactly! What they want, but no one asked what I want and this," I say, gesturing wildly about. "This is not what I want at all."

Milo sighs heavily and runs his hand through his perfectly styled hair. It falls back into place immediately as he once again looks away, averting his eyes as he turns around and paces the tent a few times.

"What are you planning on doing?" he asks. "Someone will track you down, I don't think Patrick or Robbie or your parents will let you off that easily."

"They can't make me do anything I don't want to do, you know that."

"This isn't a game, we're not kids anymore. We're adults, heirs of our families with expectations and responsibilities that we can't get out of."

"Sure, we can, we'll handle it like we always do. We've always had each other's back and we can do anything together. Just you and me and the world, we can do this. I know it! We just need to get out of this tent without anyone noticing and by the time they come looking for us, we'll be long gone. I talked to this girl I met today and she told me about open interviews being held..."

"No."

"... being held for the land train... wait, what? No?"

"I can't go with you," Milo says softly.

I don't know where his hands are, but I feel my own fly out and grab his shoulders, forcing him to look at me.

"Of course you can. You have to..."

"I... I can't. My mother and Tasha..."

My eyes grow wide as I push him roughly away.

"You don't even like Tasha," I spit at him and he turns away again, this time with his back towards me.

"I can't stop you from running, I owe you that much for being my best and only friend for so long, but I won't abandon my family so you can avoid duties to your own."

"But..." I begin, but can't think of anything to say because my brain doesn't seem to want to believe what I'm hearing. I reach out for his shoulder again, but he tenses and pulls away. Keeping his back to me, he straightens his jacket and trains his eyes forward towards the pearly pink tent. I can do nothing but stare at his back as the engagement ring on my hand feels like it weighs a hundred pounds.

"I can buy you about five minutes," says Milo. "I'll tell everyone you needed to relieve yourself before your big moment, but they'll know once they check around and can't find you. Take this too." Without turning around, he pulls his wallet from his pocket and extracts a wad of curling paper bills, which he sets on the dressing table beside him.

"I..."

"Just take it, they'll freeze your accounts again so use this to get out of Pioneer Springs as fast as you can. The longer you hang around, the more chance you'll get caught and dragged back here. Just... go."

"Not without you," I whisper and watch his shoulders begin to shake, but he doesn't turn again.

"Remember, get as far away from here as quickly as possible," he says and without another word, or a look back, he pushes the flap aside and steps outside the tent leaving me completely, and utterly, alone.

Chapter Seven

When the flap closes behind Milo, I can't help but stand there and debate my next move, but when I hear a sudden swell of music and the muttering voice of Warren swearing somewhere close by, I scurry to the back of the tent. Relief pours into me as I pull back the flap and do not notice anyone lingering around.

I still step out slowly, not wanting to risk breaking into a full out run. Much like a scared rabbit straight out of the wilds, my movements are jerky and panicked as I walk as slowly as possible by both full and empty catering tables. I pass a large table littered with discarded flower buds and the pungent and broken shards of green stems. They all remind me of myself, rejected flowers from my mother.

A large solar van stands in my way and I inch my way around the back because I can hear murmuring voices coming from the driver's seat. From the rearview mirrors, I can see someone snoring softly in the warm light while a video plays softly on a tablet before them.

I let out a breath I didn't realize I was holding and continued walking, thankful that my soft sneakers were absolutely quiet on the crabby grass and dirt patches. My dress, though, is another story as it ripples and swishes around my legs. I silently berate myself for not bringing my discarded jumpsuit, though I think my mother may have taken it with her when she left, probably to burn. There isn't anything more obvious than a runaway bride and my first item of business is to find a change of clothes as fast as possible.

More voices pop up towards the outskirts of my journey and I realize they come from a few boys I went to school with. They must have jobs as solar car drivers as part of their Required Service because they're leaning against a pair of slick back cars with red tinted hub caps. One of them is eating an apple while the other curses loudly, and they are both directly in my path and unavoidable. I slow down and hide behind a car within hearing distance of their conversation. I twirl my ring around my knuckles as I listen to their conversation.

"This was my day off," the taller one grumbles, kicking at the dusty ground.

"Mine too," the other boy says, picking at his teeth. "But what are you gonna do, huh? I hear her royal highness is getting married."

"The pig heiress?" the tall one asks. "I remember her. A bit too rich for my taste, but she can do better than that Robbie Lester."

"I fully agree with that, do you know he threw a whole sandwich at me the other day? I was five minutes late picking him up from his buddy's house and I pulled up and he just chucked the thing at my face. Right. In. My. Face. And it was one of these fully loaded things too, mustard straight into my eyes!"

"He's a piece of work, I hope he gets what's coming to him. He's going to tick off the wrong person one day," the tall one says and he looks like he would say more, but he's suddenly locked eyes with me and I realize that I was listening a little too closely to their conversation and let my cover slip.

"Um, shouldn't you be at your wedding?" the apple eating boy asks and I feel the color drain from my face.

My feet respond before I can think of something to say to him and I take off running, brushing past the tall one and making him stumble. I don't look behind, but I think I hear them laughing and maybe even cheering me on. I don't think they'll say anything, but just in case they do, I run the opposite direction of home until I'm well out of eyesight, then double back and move as quickly as my legs will carry me until I begin to recognize the dirt roads and musty air of the Bleached Fields. I'm now near the chicken mansion itself. Which means I'm not too far from home. No, I need to stop calling it that. This place is no longer my home.

The Bleached Fields run along the backside of the road where they grew probably beautiful fields full of wildflowers and butterflies once upon a time. Now the fields only grow tall white flowers that look like bleached bones in the sunlight. They had absorbed some of the toxins leaking from the Dusting, but since they were away from the main disturbance, they didn't outright die off, just adapted. I try to avoid them when I can because Patrick made me believe they were full of ghosts when we were kids. I don't have a choice today and stomp on through them. I just hope that if there are any ghosts, they will understand my plight.

My lungs begin to burn as I continue my run, which is actually more of a jog now because I've never really felt the need to train for a marathon. But just as I think I can't go any further, the back gate separating the Lester and Florence properties pops into view and I dart through it like a wild deer.

The grand house is deserted and I think Patrick and my parents must have summoned everyone to the wedding, probably as a show of power. But that's all the better for me as I dash up the stairs, taking two at a time until I slide into my room and begin ripping off the wedding dress.

As much as I hate to tear at the pretty fabric, it's a shackle that I refuse to weigh me down. It is well past five minutes and I know I don't have a lot of time left as I pull on a pair of thick jeans and a layer a black sweater over a simple pink top. I then take the wad of money from Milo and stuff it into a soft cloth backpack with a few changes of undergarments, an old flashlight and Flame's favorite romance novel she let me borrow last week.

I barely spare my room a glance before I race back out the door and am just leaving through the back gate when I make out the distinctive sound of a car screeching to a half in front of the pig mansion.

But they're too late, I'm already racing down the back paths I know will eventually lead me into town. The only person who might remember this way would be Milo and my heart aches in hope that he won't join in the hunt.

My legs, like my lungs, can't take much more and I'm forced to slow to a crawling walk. The sun is starting to set around me and clouds coming in from the west have started to bleed into those blowing in from the Dusting, painting an ombre of pinks, oranges and browns. The sky is covered so completely that there is no moon and there are no stars, only a swirling fabric of color. It is almost as if a giant unrolled a great roll of silk and flung it rippling into the air.

"You would make a stunning dress," I tell the sky and laugh at the absurdity of it all. But the laughter turns to tears soon enough and before long, I'm walking in the dark letting the tears run freely down my face because no one is around to see them.

"Flame!" I scream, pounding on the back door to Sparrow's Books, Coffee and Tea. I know I can't stay here long as this will be the first place they look, but I can't leave without saying goodbye.

"Hold your horses," I hear her mutter through the various sounds of unlocking behind the door. There is a crack in the sky and the whole world lights up in crystal light as the door swings open and I stumble inside with the rumbling thunder announcing my arrival.

"What happened to you?" Flame gasps, grabbing my elbows to hold me steady and leading me to her couch. "Why are you running around in the rain, and where is Milo?"

"I... I... Oh Flame, they were going to make me marry Robbie Lester today! Patrick must have set it up, they just tricked me into my own wedding!"

Flame's eyes open wide as I double over in racking sobs, crying into my hands. She hands me a tissue. "Did you go through with it?" she whispers.

"Of course not! I ran and ran and ran and ran, and now I'm here."

Flame looks relieved but not really happy about the situation. She squeezes my shoulders before getting up and locking the door and securing the blinds of the few windows around her tiny bedroom.

"With that dust storm, it will take them some time to track you, but I'm sure they'll be here soon," she mumbles more so to herself than to me. "Do you have a plan on what you're going to do now?"

I run my hands over my eyes and blow my nose fiercely.

"I just need a place to rest for a moment," I say, the words coming out with a trembling passion. "Then I'm going to get to this interview, I think it's the only way out of here, even if it does mean I'll have to get a job. I just need to get far away quickly before he finds me."

"Who? Milo or Robbie?"

"Both." I sniff. "Oh Flame, I asked Milo to come with me... and... and..."

"I see," says Flame, realizing what I'm trying to say. She's been my friend long enough to understand what I don't have the courage to say out loud. "It will be okay, everything always works out in the end."

"This isn't one of your romance novels."

"You're probably right, but you fit the bill nicely. You could very well be the heroine in one of them and things always work out for those girls, you'll see. Also, I don't think you're going anywhere tonight. You can barely walk and the whole city is out looking for you by now. Stay the night at least and leave for the interviews before dawn. If they catch you out there now, you'll be too weak to get away."

I can only hiccup in response and blow my nose again before giving her a hug.

"I'll make sure they don't find you, even if I have to hide you under the bed. Everything will be okay." She strokes my hair a few times and hands me a pristine book with a glossy cover before getting up to leave the room. "I've got work to finish up front, that way I can tell whoever comes looking for you that I haven't seen you. Stay back here and keep quiet."

"Okay," I whisper and she tosses me a blanket before closing and locking the door behind her.

I blow my nose one more time and huddle under the blanket by pulling it over my head and wrapping my arms around my knees. Now that my body isn't putting any thought into movement, it uses the remaining energy for thinking, remembering and fretting about the future.

They have to let me into Magenta's something or other. Maybe I can name drop the two people I met today? I don't know if they have any sway in the matter, and I don't even know what good I would be to anyone there. I've never worked a day in my life and I've never even seen a circus performance. That's two things going against me from the beginning.

I think that maybe I could lie, but I've never been good at making things up. I always seem to speak my mind and blurt out the truth sooner rather than later. No, I'll have to be honest, but not honest enough to tell them what I'm running from. If I know Patrick and my parents, they've already got a bounty out on my head and it wouldn't do me any good to come across someone willing to turn me in for the profit.

And Milo... I squeeze my eyes to stop from crying again. Flame is gone and I don't know where the rest of the tissues are and I really hate to wipe my eyes and nose on my clothes. So I squeeze them shut as hard as possible, so hard that I begin to see stars and have to open them again, but at least it works and I don't shed a tear.

I really thought he'd come with me and that we were on the same page, just like we always were before. I don't think I can fully believe that our time together meant nothing to him, but maybe I made up the narrative in my head. Maybe what I thought he felt about me was just another one of the dramatic runway shows that played endlessly in my head.

And maybe it's selfish of me, but I'm just so stunned that he would decline my offer. And for what? Tasha? Family obligations? Yuck.

Maybe I'm better off without him... No, who am I kidding? I'm not. I miss him and it hurts so much to think about going on without him.

I can hear the storm gathering intensity outside and know without looking that it's one of the bad ones that come from the Dusting. Pioneer Springs will occasionally fall prey to the boiling rains, or freezing cold winds brought about from the wild weather patterns emanating from the desolate and diseased lands just outside our border.

Sometimes they combine with actual storms, which is what sounds like is happening right now as the sounds of rain and thunder become almost deafening. I'm only just putting my hands over my ears when Flame steps back into the room. The noise is so loud that we can't even talk to each other and have to communicate with nods and smiles and frowns and shakes of our heads.

She brings with her a large tub of food, castoffs and remains from today's pastry case.

Flame lights an actual fireplace, something rare and antique, and we sit in front of it eating flaky biscuits stuffed with different kinds of jams, sugary donuts and a few ham and cheese sandwiches that Flame has already cleaned from any actual ham product.

She falls asleep quickly, perhaps lulled away by the sounds of wind and rain, but I lay awake for hours and shift around uncomfortably on her couch. The rain doesn't comfort me in the same way, it only serves as enough noise to drown out the sound of my sobs.

Chapter Eight

W e both spring awake to the tinkling sound of Flame's alarm clock playing some song I barely recognize. She leaps from her bed and after silencing the thing, she snatches the blanket away from me dramatically and stands over me like a looming tree statue.

"Come on sleepy-head, we need to head out if we're going to avoid being seen lurking about like a couple of desert wolves."

"Aren't you tired?" I croak, rubbing furiously at my eyes and she laughs, kicking me lightly with her foot.

"Not in the slightest," she says, rummaging through a pile of clothes before tossing me a large dark jacket. It is at least two sizes too big for me, but I still wear it since I know outside will be icy cold thanks to the storm.

"We need a plan before we leave," I say, trying my best to keep my voice level and calm, even though my stomach is all butterflies.

"You're right," Flame agrees and sits beside me on the couch. "Okay, for my part, I will close the shop today. I don't think anyone will bat an eyelash since the season's worst storm is still ragging away out there, that way I can help you get to the station."

"You really don't have to take me there," I say with as much firmness as I can muster. "I don't want to get you involved in this."

"Nonsense, it'll be good practice for when I finally do make it across the Dusting. Conditions there will be a whole lot worse than some muddy streets, cold rain and angry older brothers."

Sometimes I can't believe how lucky I am to have found such a good friend in Flame. I have no doubt she would follow me all the way to the glittering West Coast if I asked, but I refuse to. She has her own dreams and I will not get in the way of those desires.

"Older brother, upset parents and one jilted fiancé," I correct her and she grins.

"Patrick is no match for me and as for your parents." She pauses and then grins mischievously. "I'll throw some mud on your mom and she'll run screaming back to Swiney Acres, and your pop will follow to make sure she's alright, Robbie Lester, though? I'm not sure, but I think I can take him."

She puts her hands up as if she could be punching an imaginary Robbie in front of her and finishes with what I think must be a hard quick between the legs. She probably could hold her own.

"Seriously, though, we should get going." She puts her fists down and starts packing away a few stale pastries we didn't demolish last night.

It doesn't take long to gather a few more essentials from Flame's stash of belongings, as well as two new romance books she promises will 'knock my socks off,' whatever that may mean. It's soon time to leave the safe warm space and venture into the swirling mess that is outside, and I'm not just talking about my own predicament, the weather is absolutely hazardous now.

As soon as Flame pushes the door open, we're both assaulted with a strong wind that brings with it all manner of foul-smelling rot and decaying grass. Grit from the loose dirt leaps into our eyes, but we're quick to strap on our thick goggles that come standard with every Pioneer Springs wardrobe. Flame wraps a worn red scarf around my neck and tucks it in tightly to cover my mouth and I do the same to her. The scarf she has is one I remember making her a few years back. It's a soft beige with scribbling words set over and over again in my own swirling handwriting and each is a passage from several of her favorite, classic novels.

We gaze across the street before heading out and while it's near impossible to see through the brown colored stream of water, we don't make out any shapes resembling people. So we press on into the wind, leaning against it and making sure to keep the scarves tight around our mouths.

To get to the train station is easy, you just follow the road north and it's just at the end of town. But to get to the station during a storm is a very, very different matter. I think we're making good progress, but Flame suddenly puts her arm out and stops me from going forward and we both stare in horror down the road at the hazy, flashing red lights that can only mean the street is blocked off.

"Do you think that's for you?" Flame shouts into my ear and I can only shrug at her. It feels like something Patrick would do, but the use of local enforcement to track down one runaway bride screams Robbie Lester more.

Flame gestures at me and points off the side of the road to an abandoned building that has half collapsed in on itself. We make our way there slowly, our arms wrapped around each other's shoulders so we don't lose our way and eventually we push open the door and fall exhausted into the still and quiet lobby of what I think is the city's oldest, and most abandoned, motel.

"We're in the Flamingo." Flame exhales loudly as she pulls her scarf down below her chin and twirls around the space.

I do the same only just look around the room. The bright pink wallpaper still looks pristine, even if it hasn't been taken care of in some time.

"Cute place," I mumbled, sitting on the floor. My whole body is still exhausted and sore from my run yesterday and sleeping on Flame's couch all night certainly did not help. My muscles are screaming for some relaxation, but I know that's something that won't be coming anytime soon. The only silver lining now is that I've been so focused on moving from one thing to the next that I haven't had any time to think about what, and who, I'm leaving behind.

I'm flexing my hands and feet in thought when Flame suddenly stops her spinning and squats down beside me.

"Did you hear that?" she whispers and I turn towards her, keeping silent and listening as best I can, but all I hear is the howling of the wind outside and the stretching of some long dead tree against the old roof.

"No?" I saw unhelpfully and noticed Flame squinting towards one of the yellowed windows with a frown on her face.

That's when I heard it. There is a brief pause in the wind as the motorized sound of a large object moves down the street in front of the hotel. I can make out its vague shape through the window as it drives slowly by, the headlights bathing the whole area in dusty yellow light, and recognize the vehicle type immediately.

Whenever we have storms like this, the really bad kind that merge with the storms coming in from the Dusting, they send out these armored, square monstrosities on wheels. Someone, more often than not someone in their first year of Required Service, is made to drive up and down the streets with news and announcements. It's the most reliable source of communication since the storms tend to wipe out anything digital.

Living as an heiress, I never had to deal with those kinds of blackouts because my home had secure lines and higher priority, but I did see a few of them on the rare occasion Milo and I were caught out in the city during a sudden storm.

It's blaring a message over and over again as it moves down the street. Flame and I lean toward the window and listen carefully, but just as it passes by, we hear the message loud and clear.

"Return to your homes," it screams. "I repeat, return to your homes. The city is now in Stage Five Lockdown. You must remain in place for the duration of the storm. Required Service Interviews have been canceled, return to your homes. I repeat, go to your homes..."

The cracking sound of the speaker dims quickly as it moves from the motel and I turn to look at Flame with a face drained of color. How am I going to run away with the circus now?

Flame puts a hand on my shoulder and gives it a squeeze. My heart feels like its hardened in my chest and while my body knows I'm still breathing, I can feel the sharp edges of my shattered soul as they poke into my filling lungs

"We'll figure something out," Flame tells me, but I hardly hear her because something other than my unknown future has slid into the room. Standing in front of the flamingo wallpaper is the dirty and shaking body of the girl, Rose, whom I had met at the store with Minty and Snuzzle. She looks beat up from the storm outside and has the shadow of bruising around her left eye. And she doesn't look happy. Not at all.

"What is with this stupid city?" she yells shrilly while I fall backward against the wall opposite of her. Flame recovers more quickly and takes a more direct approach by holding out her hand.

"Let me be the first to officially welcome you to Pioneer Springs, known for the finest of shopping boutiques and literal skin-peeling storms."

"That isn't a joking matter," Rose says, spitting out black dust into the side of the room. She wipes her hand across her mouth and leans her head against the wall. "I almost died out there!"

"Here," I say, rummaging through my bag and fishing out a bottle of water. She tentatively takes it from me and takes a long drink, closing her eyes in the process. When she opens them again, I can see they are the same color as a lion statue I once saw in a shop, a stunning jade green with golden lines twirling within.

"Is it always this awful here?" Rose asks, handing the bottle back but I wave at her to keep it.

"Yes and no," Flame answers. "This storm is particularly bad and we haven't had one like it in some time. Rumor has it that the land's changing somewhere out in the Dusting proper and things are... shifting west."

"Which means more storms are mixing with the ones we already have out here," I finish for her. "That's why it's so terrible. Here, try this."

I hand her a stick of gum, but it isn't just any kind of gum. It's the kind the city gives out in ever restaurant, shop and school. A processed chewy, little stick that sucks the grim from your mouth after a few chews and leaves a soothing flavor of mint. You just have to spit it out sooner than you think or else it absorbs all the moisture in your mouth and makes you cough for several minutes. I tell Rose this and she spits it out into a napkin she pulls from her pocket and gives me what I think is a genuine smile.

"Thanks, I needed that," she says.

"How'd you end up out here at this hour?" Flame asks from my side and we watch Rose shuffle on her feet a few times.

"I, um, met someone last night... or was it early this morning? I'm not sure because after we chatted for a bit and he bought me some food, I kind of lost track of time." Her face flushes and she turns a blank gaze out the dusty windows. "By the time I realized he wasn't worth my time and started to head back to the train, I got caught up in this mess. I need to get back before the train leaves."

"Do you think it's true that they've canceled the Required Service interviews?" I ask, unable to keep the hope from leaking through my voice.

"I dunno," Rose says. "But they'll pull out of the station as soon as they can. I'm sure this kind of storm activity took everyone by surprise. Well, not Magenta and maybe not Supper, but it definitely caught me off guard. I'll be happy to get out of here as soon as humanly possible."

"Me too," I mutter, sitting back down and leaning against the wall. I wrap my arms tightly around my legs and stare distantly out the same window as Rose. Flame sits down beside me and puts her arm around my shoulder to which Rose lifts an eyebrow.

"What's wrong with you?" she asks and I turn to look at her but find I can't speak. The words keep catching painfully in my throat.

"She also needs to get out of town quickly," Flame answers for me and Rose squats beside us and peers closely into my eyes.

"Hmm," she titters, looking me up and down. "If you can get me back on through that mess and to the train, I can get you on."

"Really?" I find myself jumping back up, but Flame rises slowly and rocks on her heels before scanning Rose with a critical eye.

"Are you sure? They said the interviews were canceled," she says.

"Here maybe, but that doesn't mean they will be canceled in the next town over. You hitch a ride and hop out at the next town and interview there. Easy."

"Well, you're making it sound easy, but..." Flame doesn't look convinced, so I turn and hold both my friend's hands.

"I'll be okay, this is probably my only shot at this. I'll walk after that thing on foot if I have to. I can't go back..."

Flame nods and I know she understands I can't go back there to be the pig heiress married to Robbie Lester. She's smart though, and has read more romance novels than there are days in the year so I know she also understands that I can't go back and face the other man in my life. Milo's rejection still burns fresh in my heart, and I can never go back there. I can't be around him anymore. I clutch my stomach at the painful thought.

"You in?" Rose asks and extends her hand in the way I've seen my family do many times when making business deals. I take it and shake it up and down three times before letting go, just like Patrick and my father.

"I'm in, let's get out of this pig scat town."

Chapter Nine

"You sure about this?" Flame asks again as she helps secure my bag snugly across my shoulders. While I've left her some snacks, it's still packed tightly with clothes and the money from Milo. She then taps at my engagement ring, which I slide off my finger and secure tightly around my wrist with one last wayward ribbon.

Rose is watching intently as I turn around and hug Flame fiercely. "As sure as you are about traveling across the Dusting," I say and she smiles brightly.

"You know me so well." She sighs dreamily and gives the bag's strap one more adjustment. "And just think of all the discarded and forgotten books I'll find along the way, so many lost stories to be collected and brought to the people."

"I'll miss you so much, but I'll write as soon as I can and let you know I'm safe," I promise her with one more bone-crushing hug, which she returns easily. "Don't leave until you get a letter from me."

"I doubt I'll be able to hitch a ride across anytime soon. That probably won't be until the next chapter of my life."

"We need to get going," Rose says from the doorway. She's been equipped with Flame's set of goggles and with her wild copper hair, she looks as if she stepped straight out of a dystopian romance novel. Flame even tied the scarf I made for her around her neck and asked Rose to give it to me once we were safe inside the train. I almost felt bad that she was giving something like that to a stranger, but then I remembered how many other articles of clothing I'd made for her throughout the years and realized the scarf would end up a token of our friendship after we'd parted.

"Make sure she gets out of here," Flame warns her. "Or I will find you."

Rose rolls her eyes in response and taps her foot impatiently against the ground. I turn once more to Flame and grip her hands.

"You sure you'll be okay here?" I know she can't follow us, or even leave this place until the storm passes. It would be too dangerous outside without a pair of goggles.

"I've got several backlogged books to read and pass the time with, plus some snacks and no one around to bother me. I'll be more than fine."

I give her one last hug and make her promise to check in on little Mary once in a while and after shedding a few more tears, I join Rose by the door.

"Alright, listen carefully. Before I open this door, you need to make sure that scarf is tied tight around your face, we'll need to filter the air as much as possible. You don't want to breathe too much of it in or it will make you really sick. Keep the goggles on too, that grit out there will tear your eyes apart and roll down your sleeves to help protect your hands, it will help with the stinging."

"You all live like this around here?" Rose asks, rewinding her scarf to fit more snugly across her neck.

"You get used to it," I tell her, readjusting my goggles for a tighter fit. "We used to get these storms all the time when I was little, but they weren't as bad. Now they come less frequently but much more violently." I shrug at her. "I don't think anyone knows why."

"Well, it's a terrible way to live," Rose mutters before wrapping the scarf around her lips and waggling her eyebrows at me.

Before wrapping my own scarf, I turn once more to Flame and she gives me a brave smile. She has already set up a nice little station for herself in the corner complete with a bag of chips, a comfortable blanket, a crisp, and a new novel with a picture of what I think is a picture of a snowman.

"Flame, tell Milo..." I begin, but the words leave me and I don't know what I want her to tell him. I feel like I should have her tell him something, it would be wrong to leave a friendship like that so suddenly and awkwardly. But what is there to say?

"I'll think of something for you," Flame says gently and I do my best to keep from crying. I wouldn't be able to dry my eyes through the goggles.

"Okay, here we go." I reach for Rose's hand and she grips mine much more tightly than I would consider her capable of. I open the door to the howling maw outside.

Flame stands nearby to close it behind us and within seconds, we're shut out of the cozy and warm, flamingo themed lobby. The contrast outside is stunning in a bad way and it takes a few moments for us both to adjust our breathing to the biting air, then holding Rose's hand firmly, I begin to trudge forward until I find the sidewalk just outside the motel.

I point down at the paving stones and wait until I perceive a nod from Rose before starting down along them, never letting go of her hand. It would be bad news to get separated in a storm like this. I could probably find my way to the land train station, but she would be lost to the wilds.

We continue walking for what feels like an hour, but is probably only half that and from out of the dusty gloom, a tall building begins to glow steadily in front of us. The hazy air makes it hard to see any detail, but windows along the side glow in undulating squares of light.

Before we get close to the monster in the dim morning, I make Rose stop and catch her breath. I've had some practice breathing through a thick layer of scarf, but I know this is probably something completely new to her.

When I'm satisfied that her breathing has somewhat returned to normal, I lean into the wind and begin walking again. We finally make it to the grand entrance. The swinging doors have been boarded shut to protect them from the wind, but a smaller side door remains unlocked and we both stumble inside. As we collapse in an exhausted heap on the floor, a small electronic beeping noise begins above us and I turn to see a singular black orb set in the ceiling. It means we're being watched, or that someone at least could have the capability of watching us through the surveillance video. I kick the door shut with my feet and try not to think about it.

"That was wild!" Rose exclaims, pulling her scarf below her chin and turning to look behind her.

"Just another day in Pioneer Springs," I mumble dryly before rising and pointing to the far end of the deserted lobby. "We need to get over there, there's a door leading to..."

"Bluebell Florence, you spoiled brat, I knew I'd find you here!" a voice bellows at us from several floors above and I look up in horror to see the stern face of none other than my once bodyguard Warren, as he cranes his bulging neck over the railing to get a good look at us. "You're coming with me back to the Lesters!"

"I will most certainly not be doing that, Warren," I shout back at him. "And if you knew me, which I would think you would by now, you know you can't make me do anything I don't want to do." Then for good measure, I stick my tongue out at him, which brings an enormously loud laugh from Rose.

"Who is that?" she asks, wiping a tear from her eye as she watches Warren scurry around the floor above trying to find a way down. All too soon he finds a set of stairs and begins to descend them two at a time to get to us.

"Come on, we need to get out of here and I'll tell you on the way!" I yelp, grabbing her hand and hauling her after me.

The land train station is huge and very, very tall. While the center is a massive lobby with chairs and seats, peppered with vendor stalls and various solar charging stations, the sides rise upwards in a series of open floors, each leading out to platforms to accommodate the many different heights of land trains. The whole place feels like being inside a giant pyramid.

We find a set of stairs leading upwards and I'm turning to ask Rose if she knows what level her train's entrance would be on, when I feel her heels grind to a halt. It causes our hands to break and I look back at her in confusion, but she's staring with a wild panic in her eyes out the closest window.

"What is it?" I ask, but she's quiet as she stares out the window.

I turn to look and can make out the side of the great land train that must belong to the circus and since it's protected by the different gates and walls, the paneled sides are easy to make out. But that also makes it easy to tell that the whole thing is starting to inch forward very slowly.

"Bluebell!" Warren's voice echoes closer now and I know he'll catch up with us soon.

Rose curses loudly and turns to the nearest door, darting through it without waiting for me. I spin on my heels and hurry to match her pace, but she's too quick and before long, I see her make it to a small side door far ahead of me on the crawling train. She pulls it open and leaps inside, thankfully leaving it open behind her. All I can see now is the side of her hand as she waves, but I don't know if she's waving goodbye or telling me to hurry up.

Ignoring the new beeping noise above the door, I start running but just as I take off, something clamps down on my back and hurls me to the side. My shoulder jolts painfully on the hard ground and my bag slides off my shoulders. Crying out in pain, I'm scrambling to right myself when something thin and sharp cuts into my neck. It draws blood instantly and I feel it trickling down my collarbone as my assailant leans close to my ears. I expect it to be Warren, but my heart sinks when I recognize the voice of my jilted fiancé. Robbie's crazed expression becomes blurry as tears of pain spring to my eyes.

"Hold still, you know what this is. One too many moves and it'll hurt much more than it already does," Robbie breathes into the side of my neck. My skin crawls at his closeness, but I resist lashing out.

"Robbie, please," I whimper. "Don't do this."

He tightens the wire and I don't even know why, maybe just for fun. I squeal in pain while my neck is hot with blood, but I hold my ground and stay as still as possible.

"I already sounded the alarm, everyone should be here soon enough and all you have to do is come quietly with me," he growls lowly. "We'll get this ceremony over with and then I can lock you back up in your mansion, and it'll all be over. I won't let you embarrass me again."

I shift the slightest inch and feel the wire digging deeper into my skin. My eyes scan the area, trying to find a way out of this but all I see is the train creeping away, the open door and the surveillance camera's red glow above. Wild thoughts of escape run through my mind, but I can't hold onto any of them and I have no idea how to get out of this. My eyes begin to tear up again and through them the only thing I see now is the giant train inching further and further away from me.

Suddenly there is a loud cracking noise and I feel Robbie's weight shift onto me, crushing me to the ground. He's a dead weight on top of me, but the wire has thankfully gone slack and fallen to the ground in a pool of splattering blood. Someone kicks it away before using their foot to shift a moaning Robbie from me. I try to get up, but find my knees buckle beneath me. However, a familiar hand reaches down in front of my face.

I look up to see Milo's concerned expression as he takes in the ravished skin of my neck. He holds a solid-looking baton loosely at his side. Letting him hoist me up, I find the train hasn't moved that far and another door has been propped open as a beacon of hope towards the tail end, which only now is quickly approaching.

Milo sees it too and steps over Robbie who is now struggling to get back up. He gives me a stiff and quick embrace before letting me go and stepping beside Robbie. He then delivers a swift kick that sends him sideways to the ground once more.

"Get on before I change my mind and take you back to your parents," Milo says, but I find moving too hard right now because I'm trapped by the painful look in his eyes.

"Come with me," I please once more, but he shakes his head.

"You know I can't."

"But what are you going to do about that?" I ask, pointing at Robbie's writing body. I have to actually swallow a scream when I see Robbie finally succeed in standing up and leveling a murderous glare in my direction.

"I've dealt with worse," Milo says and I stare at him blankly, wondering how and why that could be true.

"You little..." Robbie begins, but Milo silences him with another swift hit of his baton. It sends him to the floor where he remains motionless.

But there's no time to think and wonder about what happened before or what could happen if I stay. The last open door is just within reach and now is my only chance, so I grab hold of a small handlebar and swing my body into the open doorway, staring back at Milo as he steps over Robbie's body and blocks him from my view. The surveillance camera flashes above him and I wonder how much it saw, but the thought is muted against the realization that this might be the last time I see Milo.

"Goodbye, Bluebell," he calls sadly. "I wish you nothing but the best out there in the, uh, west."

"Such a lame farewell," I yell back, but it comes out as more of a choking sound when he gives me a watery smile. The train suddenly picks up speed and I have to grab hard onto the rail to keep from falling out.

He waves to me once more as the monstrous giant I cling to picks up speed and even though there is no way Milo can hear me now, I tell him goodbye.

Chapter Ten

M ilo's form grows small as the train leaves the station and I have no choice but to look away and focus on securing the doorway. Closing a door on a moving train is much harder than I anticipated, but after throwing my shoulders into it and struggling for a few minutes, I manage to get the thing shut against the howling air. It cuts off and leaves me in a stuffy, warm room filled with piles of boxes.

Exhausted I fall against the door frame and am attempting to catch my breath when I hear someone calling to me from across the expansive room I've found myself in.

"Oh good, you found the other door," says Rose as she walks over, dodging various crates and containers and stopping a few feet away when she notices my bleeding neck. "Oh, ew, that looks bad."

I touch it gingerly and grimace when my fingers come back with dried blood. At least it's not actively bleeding. I wind my scarf tightly around just in case, but now it will need to be cleaned up as soon as possible. I don't relish the scar it will also leave behind as a lasting memory of my so-called bodyguard's protection.

I look up to see Rose standing in the middle of the room picking at her nails and looking bored.

"So, what now?" I ask, not even attempting to get up.

She shrugs and gestures around her. "Wait around here and when the train stops moving, get out before anyone sees you. Then you can interview for the Required Service there and hope they take you on."

Her words are chilling because I never thought about what to do if they didn't accept me into their program, but I nod all the same and give her a weak smile as she walks away. She flips her hair over a shoulder and gives the room a look of disgust.

"You should be fine in here. There's only one guy I know who comes down this far, but he won't notice you unless you crawl out on all fours looking for some milk or something."

"What are you talking about?" I ask her, but she waves me off.

"If you hear the door open, just hide and you'll be fine. There's plenty of places to hide in this dump."

"You make it sound so pleasant," I grumble.

"Don't worry, it's not pleasant at all. Anyway, thanks for getting me back on board, I'll be back to check on you later!" she calls over a shoulder before quickly exiting through a narrow doorway I hadn't noticed until now. It stands between two large stacks of boxes and doesn't look locked, but there is no way I would go through it without knowing what was on the other side.

"Wait, what is..." I start to ask, but she's gone so quickly that I end up talking to an empty room.

I cannot believe she just left me here. After meeting Minty and Snuzzle, I thought people in the circus would be pleasant. I guess I was wrong about that. I'm also still not entirely convinced she didn't intend to leave me behind to my fate.

As the door closes behind her, I realize she never returned Flame's scarf to me and while it irks me to have forgotten to remind her, I make a mental note to get it back from her when I see her next. I guess I do know where she works, after all.

The land train gives a lurch under me, but I risk standing up to at least move myself away from the doorway and work my way further into the room. There aren't any windows here, but slivers of morning light leak through various vents cut into the walls and from them I can make out the quickly moving terrain. I think I might even see the Bleached Fields somewhere in the distance, but it's hard to tell for sure. There could be other barren and diseased places out that I just don't know about.

Everything in here is either embossed with Cloudspeak Corporation logos, the most popular brand in the country today, or with the words Magenta's Magical World of Circus Curiosities, which I gather is the name for everyone in this traveling beast. I think Minty or Snuzzle may have said as much, but it feels like ages ago when I was speaking with them inside Theo's Threadshop. Was it really just yesterday?

I shake my head trying to clear the jumbled thoughts, but they fall back helplessly. I need to get back into a daily routine, this runaway bride stuff really isn't setting a stable footing for my mental clarity.

"But at least I'm free," I find myself whispering to the air. It whispers back and tells me that it doesn't care and reminds me of the stinging sensation around my neck. Sighing deeply I venture to the center of the room and take a seat on one of the crates. It's a little high and my feet dangle from it as if I were Mary's age.

No, I can't think about her right now.

So, I instead think about Rose's words regarding the interviews as they linger in my brain and make me wonder what the process is even like. What kinds of questions do they ask? What would I have to share about myself that doesn't involve being a spoiled and rich pig heiress? I know some stuff about pigs... would that count? If anything, maybe they would let me work in the kitchens.

But Flame's suggestion to skip out as soon as possible and use the money I could get from the engagement ring to get far away is probably my best option. No matter how tempting staying in the circus might be. The Lesters and my family are sure to come looking for me here once they figure out I'm no longer in town.

Thinking about Robbie and my escaped marriage makes the ring feel heavier than usual and I slowly unwind it from my wrist and tuck it deep into my pocket. Out of sight, out of mind.

I then realize I don't even know what city the train is headed towards and I get up from the crate and make my way to the slivers of daylight streaming through the walls. There is one at just the right height for me to stand beside and stare outwards. I watch the countryside as it flashes by, but it's too quick to make out any details and actually all looks like the same golden blur. It makes my head spin trying to watch it, so I step away into the cool darkness of the storage room.

Trying to shake off the feeling of nausea, I begin wandering around the room and examining the crates and boxes that line the walls. Most of it is mundane, just boxes of clothes and worn-out shoes, even a box full of faded fashion magazines that are mostly yellow with age. I can barely make out the pictures from them but they look like catalogs of old costumes, as if someone had been keeping a meticulous record of who wore what and when.

There are pages of colorful clothing in them, bright and floppy hats that are works of art and beautiful to look at. I flip to a page in one and find a stunning young woman wearing a long navy dress with a train that looks like it could be at least fifty feet long. Someone has studded the fabric with diamond like beads to create what looks like a nighttime sky. Even the woman's hair, which is massive and curly and round, is studded with the same crystals and she appears to wear a whole galaxy atop her shoulders.

I clutch the magazines to my chest because they're too beautiful to leave behind to gather dust and also pull a few more out that I stack in a small pile to the side. It seems obvious to me that no one wants them, and that like me, they've been discarded and left behind in this storage room. I doubt anyone will miss them.

I pick up the pile and bind them gently together with a stray ribbon I found still tied to my hair. I'm turning to place them snugly inside my already full bag, but break out into a cold sweat when I realize it's not here.

Then I remember fighting with Robbie and how he had pulled me backward so forcefully that my bag had slipped off my shoulders.

My core seems to contract within itself and I crumple to the floor clutching my sides. I left my bag at the station. It could still be sitting there on the ground beside Robbie's spilled blood unless Milo took it.

No, I can't think about either of them. Robbie, because he very well could be dead right now and Milo, out of the guilt he may have gotten himself into big trouble by helping me leave Pioneer Springs.

The biggest weight on my mind is that the bag with all my stuff, my clothes, the books from Flame and all the money is gone. Left behind and forgotten just like the photos in my hand.

I have no way to tell what time it is, Milo was the one who always wore a watch and controlled where I needed to go and when. So now, alone in this storage room with little to no light, the only indication that the day is moving swiftly to night is how the temperature drops dramatically.

My stomach growls and it's getting hard to swallow, but I maintain hope that the only person who knows I'm here will bring back some food and water. That is, unless Rose has already forgotten about me.

Shivering from the biting air, I rummage through another of the crates and find a few blanket-like robes that I use to create a nest for myself in the room's corner, protected by several of the larger boxes. I curl up inside and try not to think about what the wedding cake for my impromptu wedding must have tasted like.

Milo surely told them how much I like strawberry, so I could imagine it was filled with custard laced with sliced berries, maybe there was even a chocolate drizzle available on the side. There would have been sparkling juice and wine, and it would have been catered with more pork and chicken products than I care to think about.

"Why is this place so stinking cold," I say to no one but myself as I shift around in my blankets. While the cracks between the walls allow some light from the setting sun to leak inside, they thankfully do not let in too much cold air. But a barren, non-insulated storage room at the bottom of a speeding land train is not designed for an overnight stay.

As peckish and thirsty as I am, there is another problem that I've become increasingly aware of, my beck is burning. While it's long stopped bleeding, it feels swollen and painful and I can tell it needs to be cleaned and taken care of soon.

But what can I do? I don't have anything with me and rummaging through the crates provided fruitless, there isn't anything to eat or drink here and I don't want to risk using any of the aged cloth against my neck. The only thing I had was my scarf, which I tied in an uncomfortable knot around my throat and hoped for the best.

It's bad enough that I start fantasizing about how it would have been to stay behind. Would the wedding have been so bad? Probably not, it was the afterwards that I wasn't looking forward to. Maybe I should have just gone through with it and then run away afterwards? But this land train would have been long gone and who knows when another opportunity like this would come along. Plus, I would be married, and that might prove a whole new set of problems because Robbie Lester may have very well followed up on the promise of locking me in my room.

But I would have been around to keep an eye on Mary, maybe get lucky and drink coffee with Flame and read scandalous romance novels with her. I could be walking down the streets with Milo and sharing tofu bites with him in the evenings. No, even if I did stay, Flame would leave to travel across the Dusting and I could never, ever, ask her to stay with me. And Milo would have his own marriage to stupid Tasha. Mary would grow up one day and I would still be left alone to deal with the hateful Lesters.

I soon become accustomed to the lurching of the train and the undulating motion helps to lure me into a trance as I stared straight ahead of me, trying not to think about everything and waiting for Rose to show back up. But as time ticks by and I find that I'm still alone, the tears start to brim in my eyes and burn their way down my face and irritate my broken skin.

A fitful and absolutely awful sleep comes for me at some point, but something else finds me in the night and I wake to a soft little thing squirming against my side. I look down and find a tiny grey and white kitten. Her eyes are still sealed shut in that helpless kitten like way, but she rolls around on a fat little belly and presses her tiny paws into my skin wherever she can.

Startled, I look down and just as I'm wondering where she came from, an adult cat who must be her mother trots over and deposits another kitten next to her. This one is bigger and all black. Their soft cries and rolly bellies bring on a watery smile.

"You guys are so much cuter than the piglets back at Swiney Acres," I find myself cooing at them. "Stay close and we'll keep each other warm."

Before long, the mother cat, who is a stunning tawny brown color, has brought over a total of five babies to my side. She curls up beside them, barely sparing me a second glance, before settling in to let them nurse.

Outside the land train's walls must be an icy landscape of flashing countryside, but you would never know it from the warm and peaceful scene in here. Sleep comes for me again and wrapped in my found blankets and listening to the softly purring mother cat, I drift off into a dreamless abyss.

Chapter Eleven

Something sharp pokes my hand and wakes me up, and I open my eyes to two large, glowing green orbs. The mother cat impatiently pats my hand a few more times until I lift it slowly and scratch her behind her ears. Her kittens sleep neatly in a pile beside her, all tucked inside their own little nest of blanket. They actually look really cute and I love how each one is a different color, so unlike the small wiggling pink piglets I'm used to seeing.

"I don't suppose you know where I can find something to drink?" I question as she continues to stare at me with unblinking green eyes. She stretches lazily and curls up beside her kittens and I lay down as well, watching their tiny bodies breathe.

Somewhere beneath us, the train is moving at a speed I cannot even comprehend. I've watched a few races from the faster solar cars, but I feel like they would in no way compare to the quickness of this moving giant. The town of Pioneer Springs must be far, far behind us.

Eventually, my other needs rouse me and I scan the small room once more, looking for something, anything, that could be used as a toilet. But when my search comes up with nothing, I find myself standing in front of the door I saw Rose use yesterday.

I'm scratching at my irritated neck when the mother cat joins me at the door, rubbing all about my legs in a swirling figure eight pattern. I lean down to pet her again, but the moment brings on a fresh wave of sickness and reminds me again of my need to relieve myself.

"Come on, Bluebell. You can do this," I mutter to myself. The cat cocks her head to the side at my raspy voice and gives me a small trill of encouragement when I creak the door open as slowly as possible.

What meets my eyes is both disappointing and exciting. It's another storage room, but this one seems to contain an extremely small, corner restroom that has been sectioned off into a basic toilet and washing sink. I stumble over to them and the mother cat has to dart away from my trembling legs. After relieving myself and guzzling water straight from the sink tap, I splash the rest on my face and feel almost normal. I then scoop a small amount into my hands and bend down to offer it to the pretty feline by my feet, but she turns up her nose at my offering. Typical cat.

Not wanting to spend too much time in this unknown room, I return to my nest of blankets and sit down. While my thirst may have been parched, there is still the issue of not having had any-thing to eat in some time. Then as if in response to even thinking about food, my stomach gives out a loud grumble that wakes the sleeping kittens. They begin to crawl around blindly on their fat little bellies and the mother cat settles in eagerly to offer them a meal.

Trying not to think about food and keeping my focus on more clinical and boring things like the difference between baby cats and baby pigs, I feel myself begin to drift off. My eyes are heavy as I curl up beside the small family. Soon, both myself and the cats are taking a little cat nap.

That is, until I hear the door to the storage room creaking open.

Startled awake, I bolt upright and lean against the wall, hoping that if I remain still enough whoever it is will be on their way soon and won't look too carefully inside. However, the mother cat has other intentions.

She sits up straight and I see her again tilt her head to the side as if she were directing one of her perfectly pointed and big ear towards the dooryard. Then, satisfied with who knows what, she nudges her kittens together into a small pile and trots off toward the doorway.

She's greeted by a deeper mumbling voice and I know right away that it is not Rose. Terrified of being discovered, I look around at my few options for hiding but see nothing. I don't even think I could dart inside a nearby box without toppling one of the kitten piles next to me. As sweet as the little things are, I'm sure they could be as loud as piglets if disturbed.

My hands begin to sweat as I stand up, preparing myself to perhaps run deeper into the train to look for a better hiding spot, or maybe I could sweat talk my way out of this. I used to be able to think of all kinds of excuses to get out of social situations Milo and I found ourselves in, maybe I could...

"Oh, look what the cat dragged in," the deep voice chuckles, now suddenly in front of me. If there was any flight or fight in me, it rapidly disappears at the stupid phrase and unable to hold my tongue, I find myself responding instead of feeding.

"What a stupid thing to say from..." I scanned the newcomer a few times. "From a clown?"

He gives me a cocky smile and bends into a mocking bow that is almost endearing because when he rises to meet my eyes, I see they are a bewitching deep blue. His hair is the color of fresh straw and he has to be at least as tall as Milo, but with a more slender build. But while attractive enough to be on the cover of one of Flame's romance novels, he is also wearing an oversized, brown suit jacket with a multitude of patchwork squares in every color of the rainbow.

"You have me pegged, ma'am. I used to be a tumbler, but found that I'm much too lazy to be practicing all the time for something as silly as flying through the air."

"I see," I say, unsure of what to make of him. He certainly looks strong, though I have no idea what a tumbler could be. That jacket, though, he must be in some sort of comedy act. Pity... I bet he has some nice muscles hiding under those weird clothes...

But while I debate who this insanely attractive man is and if he could be a threat to my security, the mother cat peers around the corner and begins to wind herself around his legs several times before jumping onto his shoulders and rubbing her head against his cheek.

"Snowy," he purrs at her as if he were a cat himself. "There you are."

I watch as the mother cat nuzzles her face into his neck and returns the purring, then clear my throat and point down at the blanket nest.

"You probably mean, 'there they are,'" I say, gesturing at the pile of now wide-awake kittens wiggling around like tiny, furry potatoes.

"Oh," he says, kneeling down and turning an eye at his cat. "I figured you went somewhere private for this, but can't imagine how you got locked up down here. No one uses these storage room entrances for good purposes." He turns an eye to me and I cross my arms defensively across my chest as he says, "But it looks like you found some good company."

I squint my eyes at him and he extends a hand that looks rough with small scratches.

"Clive," he introduces himself. "And who exactly are you?"

I take Clive's hand and shake it in the way I've seen my mother greet the ladies from town, which is a firm grip with only twice up and down, then making sure to let go first. But while I do this, I can't take my eyes off his until I clear my throat awkwardly and look away.

"Bluebell," I tell him. He didn't say his last name so I don't feel the need to volunteer my own. Who knows how far my family's pig kingdom spans.

"Well, from the looks of you, I'd say you were one of the new Stage Girls we picked up at that last stop, but somehow I don't think that's it," Clive says and just as if we were old friends, he slides down the wall and sits down beside his cat family.

I don't want to be weird and talk down to him, so I kneel down carefully as well. When I do, the smallest kitten who is a tawny orange color, waddles towards me and begins to snuggle against my leg. I pick him up gently and deposit him with his brothers and sisters at the mother cat's side, but make sure to pet his little head just a tiny bit before letting go.

"What makes you say that?" I ask him.

"Well, first off, no one comes down here unless they're sneaking on or off this thing when we're stopped and it looks like you got on and haven't left, so I'm assuming you don't have anywhere to go onboard and are what they call 'a stowaway.' Also... um, is your neck bleeding?"

I lift a finger to touch my scarf and it smudges my fingers with blood. The mother cat lifts her face and sniffs at the air while Clive leans in for a better look. I instinctually lean away from him, but I don't think he means any harm as he pulls away with a concerned look on his face.

"That looks bad," he says softly, rising to his feet. "We should get that taken care of."

"I... can't. I should stay here, at least until we get into the next town."

Clive shifts on his feet and offers me his hand. "That won't be for a day or two and that looks like it needs attention now. Come on, I know just the person who can help."

"But I..."

"How about this?" H takes his quilted jacket off and then after draping it across my shoulders, he begins to fill up the colorful squares, which I see now are pockets, with the kittens.

The mother cat sits nearby with an amused look to her features, if cats can even have emotions like people, but she doesn't protest as he fills the jacket pockets up with the tiny squirming babies.

"What are you doing?" I say and can't help but smile.

"No one is going to kick you off the train if it looks like you're full of kittens," he says matter-of-factly and flashes me a heart melting smile.

Clive seems like the strangest person I've ever met, but he's also extremely good looking and seems to have a good heart. He just has a warming and safe presence around him, something I haven't noticed from anyone else besides Milo.

"I guess not?" I say back uncertainly and give a small laugh which makes his whole face brighten.

"Golly, you're really pretty when you laugh," he says.

"Who says 'golly' anymore," I can't help but reply and he chuckles in return and points towards the door.

"Come on, I'll take you to my friend, Sal."

"Who is that?" I ask and he shrugs his shoulders.

"Just a friend and fellow animal lover. She knows a thing or two about taking care of them too. I need to take these babies over for her to take a look at anyway, so it's not like taking you to her would be out of the way." He smiles to let me know he's joking.

"So, you're taking me to see a veterinarian?"

"I sure am, doll face, so let's get going before one of those kittens makes a mess inside my coat. Oh, and you didn't by any chance see another, bigger cat around here, did you? Black and white?"

I shake my head, remembering only the mother cat and her babies.

"Oh well, I'll get him one day. You aren't the only stowaway on board, there's another cat somewhere here that I haven't been able to find yet." He shrugs his shoulders, which I can see are broad and expansive with that hidden kind of muscle, and gives me a heart melting smile as he gestures me to follow him.

The wiggling potatoes have quieted and a few are softly making little biscuits with their paws, but I still find myself moving very slowly so I don't disturb them. Clive makes a soft whistling sound and the mother cat, whose name he tells me is Snowbird, jumps on his shoulders for a free ride.

Before leaving, I take a little care to fold the blankets back up and place them neatly in an empty crate. Then I collect my pile of magazines and find a pocket large enough to hold them within Clive's jacket and keep them close. Clive eyes them as I do so.

"This is one of the lesser used storage rooms," he says and waves his hand around the room. "We're on the lowest of the low levels too, near the back end. You can't get much more out of the way than this."

I nod along as he continues to talk about the land train, but find myself beginning to tune out his words the deeper inside we travel. We haven't come across any other humans, though we do walk by a large black cat grooming his whiskers to which Clive greets as if he were human.

"Lots of mousers down here," he explains. "None of the performers, though, they stay up with me."

"Performers?"

"Ah, yes, my act," he says and even though I'm walking behind him, I can see the way the back of his neck flushes. "Like I said, the tumbler life wasn't for me, but my family has always been circus and it's in my blood. So, if I wasn't going to follow in their footsteps, I had to do something."

"I see, so what exactly is that something?" I ask as we arrive a small lift elevator. I stand just outside of it and I'm not sure if it's because I don't want our conversation to end or if I'm afraid of going deeper into the belly of the beast.

"Clowning," says Clive, turning to me with a big smile. "Well, sort of like clowning. I guess it really bridges the gap between clowning and some of the more niche performance acts, but I perform silly little acts with my cats to warm up the circus crowds pre-show."

"I've never seen someone do an animal act," I tell him honestly, fighting with the hem of my shirt. "I don't even know what that would be like. My experience with animals has all been pig related and they're smart, but maybe not as endearing as something cute and furry."

Clive nods in understanding.

"It's hard to watch your food dance for your entertainment before you turn around and consume it."

"Exactly! I actually don't eat any kind of meat. It just doesn't seem right," I tell him and Clive nods sagely.

"You'll like it here then. Plenty of meat-eaters around, including the cats, but Magenta isn't keen on animal proteins, so the vege-tarianism just sort of trickles down."

"Sounds great to me," I say, feeling my face brighten at the prospect of not being judged for my meal choices, but it also makes the knots inside grow tighter and I turn to Clive before taking a step into the waiting lift.

"Is this, um, safe? What happens if I get caught? Do you think they'll still let me interview for the Required Service if they catch me hiding out in here?"

Clive runs his hand over his mouth and eyes my neck, which has started to burn as it rubs against the crusty scarf.

"I don't know if you have any other choice," he says softly.

I sigh and feel my shoulders sink in defeat, but still take a deep breath anyway and follow him inside the lift. He's right, what other choice do I have? The lift doors close behind me and we're alone in the small, cramped space. Well, unless you count the six cats with us.

Once I feel the floor moving beneath me, Clive looks down at me and gives me a weak smile.

"I haven't been completely honest with you," he says and I feel the hairs on the back of my neck stand on end. "I am taking you to see Sally, but she should be with our boss, Magenta, right now. I hope you're ready for an impromptu RIS interview."

Chapter Twelve

T he lift is smooth but jolts to the side once or twice on our quick journey and I have to put my arms out to brace myself against the wall to keep from crushing my little bundles of furry potatoes. Thankfully, they're still sleeping and oblivious to the snarl I give Clive.

"Excuse me? You're taking me where?" I hiss, very much cat-like, and in another cat-like way, Clive waves my aggression off with a flip of his wrist.

"It's eleven in the morning and Magenta always comes to see the cow with Sally at this time. It's a two-for-one. I get my kittens looked at and you get to meet the main attraction herself. And as a bonus, Sally can take a look at your neck."

I feel faint and I don't know if it's from the lack of food, the quickly moving lift or the prospect of having to plead my case to someone so important when I'm in such a horrible state. Clive gives me an encouraging smile, but it's the gentle purring from Snowbird that soothes me the most.

Much to Clive's dismay, she jumps from his shoulders to settle on mine and butts her head against my ear, carefully avoiding the bloody scarf. She jumps back when Clive gives her a warning click of his tongue and tells her to be careful of my neck. Whether or not she understands is unclear, but he seems to act like she does.

I also don't want to tell Clive, or Snowbird for that matter, that staying here is not my ultimate goal, and that I plan on leaving as soon as possible. Even though I feel the ring burning in my pocket and my finger twitch as if it were still there, twirling between my knuckles.

All too soon the lift doors open and I find myself in a long mahogany colored hallway. There is even a plush carpet on the ground that may have once seen better days, but now has been trampled by the cloven hooves of some big beast.

"How did you guys even get a cow?" I ask Clive while we pick our way down the hall.

"Not sure, but rumor has it that she was won in a game of poker."

"Is it even legal to own one?" I ask, prefixed but still intrigued. I've never seen a cow up close. One or two have passed through Pioneer Springs in the past, but I was never permitted to visit them or even get close. They're heavily protected by their caretakers and the government.

"It's okay for us," says Clive. "She doesn't do much, just stands there mostly, and we charge people to get a good look at her. Not a lot of people have ever seen one in real life. I've been trying to convince Sally to let the cats ride around on her for an opening act."

"Does the cow make a lot of money?" I find myself asking.

"Not as much as I do, you'd be surprised how many people find amusement in acrobatic cats," Clive answers with a flashing smile that makes me blush and turn away. "That's why I'd love to see what they could do if combined together."

We've arrived at an ornate door with what looks to be a golden colored emblem of a cow on its handles and I can hear murmuring voices inside.

"Oh, there's more than just the cow in here. Hope you don't mind chickens," Clive says quickly as he opens the door.

"Well, I actually..." I start, but the door swings open and I'm assaulted by all the familiar fragrances of home, complete with countless and swarming white and brown birds moving at my feet.

Clive walks casually inside and gestures for me to follow. I tiptoe in, trying at first to hold my breath, but letting it go once I realize that I'll have to breathe the air eventually. I turn around to close the door and hope he doesn't see my scowl.

I suppose it isn't the chicken's fault that they remind me of bitter and angry memories, the little things didn't do anything to me personally, but I can't help the sweat pooling at the base of my back or the way my eyes go twitchy when I stare at them too long. At least there aren't any pigs in here.

"Parker? That you?" A tall woman who I am assuming is Sally looks up from the back of the extensive room and smiles when she sees Clive and me standing there.

"Oh!" She gives a girlish squeal that makes several chickens flutter away from her. "Did the kittens come?"

Clive takes my elbow and steers me towards her. She beams at him but turns a curious eye in my direction. After a curt nod from Clive, she thankfully keeps any thoughts to herself as he begins to pull the babies out from the many coat pockets. He places them into a nearby basket and hands it over to Sally. Snowbird, watching intently, gives her a wary eye as she jumps down to be with her kittens.

"You look awfully familiar," Sally mutters, looking over from the kittens to my face. I can tell she's thinking hard and searching for something recognizable in my features so I make to turn away from her and duck behind Clive, but I'm too late and see the smile speaking easily across her face.

"That's it! You're the pig girl!" she practically screams while more birds flutter wildly away.

I feel the blood rushing to my cheeks at her comment and use my hands to cover my face, but Clive reaches over and peels them away.

"What is she talking about?" he asks, more curious than anything.

"Come on," Sally teases Clive. "You're telling me you don't recognize that face, go on and look closer."

"Or don't," I say, backing up a few steps as Clive squints his eyes at me. Even in his oversized jacket, I feel as if I'm on full display as the ghost of a smile forms on his face.

"You're the bacon girl." He laughs suddenly and the sigh I let out is long and drawn out.

"Correction," I tell them, holding a finger up to his face. "My older sister was the 'bacon girl,' I just look a lot like her and I was the, um, baby on the pork and bean tin cans."

"What are the odds!" cries Sally. "A little celebrity! Well, my little pig princess, your family makes some good pork products."

"I suppose," I tell her and cross my arms against my chest, but the action irritates my neck and makes me visibly wince. Sally casts a concerned look my way and places the basket of cats on the ground.

"Something tells me that you need some attention before these fur balls," she says, gesturing for me to come closer. Clive gives me a nod when I look at him, so I take a step closer for this strange lady to take a look.

She's soon unfolding the scarf and I shrink back at the pain when it rips my skin freshly open. I stumble back, fighting the urge to black out, but Clive is there and supports my weight against his side. I'm too occupied with the pain and his warm and solid body behind me to notice when a fourth figure has stepped into view and when I finally do pay attention, I open my eyes to the most majestic looking person I have ever seen.

Standing before us is a woman who seems as tall and mighty as the biggest of the stone trees from Pioneer Springs. Her hair is a halo of curly purple-pinks and rosy reds, it circles a tan colored face with flashing and feral eyes. There is no doubt this person is in charge of not only the room, but possibly the world.

The only thing I think that could hold her back is that blazer she is wearing. I believe the color is somewhere within the yellow family, but it verges too far into orange and looks unpleasant against her darker features.

Temporarily losing myself in her wardrobe distracts me from noticing how close she steps up to me and before I know it, I'm shrinking before her powerful presence.

"My word," Magenta breathes and I'm mesmerized by the deep voice as she addresses me and gestures toward my bleeding neck. "What sadistic creep did this to you? Will you tell Magenta, hmm?"

I shake my head, not because I don't want to answer her, but because I know talking right now would be too painful. I attempt something but it comes out as a choking sound and she looks at me sadly.

"Where did you find this kitten?" she asks Clive. He shuffles his feet and doesn't answer right away, which earns him a lifted eyebrow from the looming figure of Magenta.

"Ah, I see," she says, stepping to the side so that Sally can inspect my neck. She doesn't move away and instead grabs my hands and begins to inspect my palms while Sally gets to work.

The pain radiating from my neck amplifies as Sally dabs at it with lotions and binds it snuggly with a long clean cloth that thankfully does not smell at all like chickens. She holds a finger to her lips and gives me a stern expression.

"Do not speak, eat, drink or do anything with your mouth and throat for at least half an hour," she warns. Her expression softens when she notices the look of horror that I'm sure is etched upon my face and she pats my arm. "Just give the medication time to sink in and everything will be okay. Look like it will recover smoothly, but will still leave a nasty scar I'm afraid."

Magenta finishes her inspection just after Sally and lets go of my palms. Standing to her full height before me, she looks down and into my eyes. There is something terrifying about the demeanor of this woman, as if she could stamp one of her boots and make the whole world crumble beneath her feet.

"Your palms are smooth, indicating you've been a princess at some point in your life, or possibly a person of great importance at some time. But your fingertips are hard and calloused as diamonds, showing that you do or have done work with needles and with threads and with cloth and with sharp things that poke and prod into your life."

Clive and Sally lean in and listen, and if I could move, I'd push them away from this conversation. I would rather them not see me beg. I will do what needs to be done so I don't have to go back to Pioneer Springs.

"I have experience in making clothes," I let out and Sally sighs in exasperation as Clive either hushes me or one of the kittens squirming in his hands.

"Do you?" Magenta purrs as if she too were a cat. She folds her arms across her expansive chest and tilts her head as she looks down.

"Yes, and some color theory as well. For example, that blazer looks awful on you, the color clashes terribly with both your hair and skin tone. Jewel tones, perhaps a navy blue with accents of gold, would be much more striking and create the allure it seems you're after."

Sally stares at me with her mouth open and I don't know if what I said was out of line or if she's amazed, I was able to get all those words out with such a neck injury. Clive is still and quiet, but gives me an encouraging wink when no one is looking.

"Heavenly Starlings," Magenta breathes. "I don't know where you came from, little princess, but I think you'll be able to hold your own around here. Sally or Clive, would one of you take her to Snuzzle after seeing to things here? She'll have to share a room, but I'm sure they'll manage until construction on their floor is finally complete."

"You got it, boss," says Sally and Clive gives her a lazy smile.

"Does this mean I can stay?" I ask. By now my throat is burning and I can already see Sally taking out more salve for my neck, but I have to ask. I have to know for sure.

Magenta nods and amusement flashes through her expression as she waves her hand with all the grandiose of someone who's been born on stage. She gestures to the cow, who I see is ambling nearby and looks oblivious to all of life's cruelties inflicted upon her kind. Lucky thing.

"I have a soft spot for those brave enough to be bashed about by the world and still find themselves standing among its wreckage." With that, she lifts her chin and exits the room on long elegant legs.

"Well, that went nicely," says Clive, grabbing my shoulders and in a move that would have been right at home with Milo, he gives them a firm squeeze before letting go and beaming at me.

"I guess so," I try to say, but it comes out in a terrible cough that makes me double over.

"Shush, Clive," Sally reprimands, turning back to me with more slave and a fresh bandage. "You need to keep her quiet so this can heal up, then I can finally get to your kittens."

Clive pretends to seal his lips with a lock and toss me the key. With a wink, he ducks away from us and begins reassuring Snowbird that Sally will be nice to her kittens.

As Sally works, I look down at him by my feet. He's holding one of the kittens, the fuzzy black one, in his hands and presses his forehead between the baby's ears. He mumbles something and the baby wiggles in his hands to be put back with the rest of its family as it lets out a strikingly loud cry. I don't know what was said between them, but Clive seems satisfied.

He catches me looking at him and for a moment, he's the only one in the room and I'm lost in dark blue eyes. I'd look away, but Sally is busy arranging the cloth around my neck and I know she'll be mad if I move.

"I bet you're wondering what I asked him," Clive asks from the ground and I lift my eyebrows at him in interest. "I needed to see if he would consider being in the act when he's older, I need an all black cat for an act I'm planning."

Sally laughs for me.

"You're an odd one, Clive," she says, putting away her bandages and salves into a black case. "Did you find that black and white cat yet?"

"No." He pouts, returning the little kitten to the rest of its family. "But it's only a matter of time."

Sally laughs like she doesn't believe him and then turns to look me straight in the eyes. "You need to keep quiet, no matter what nonsense this clown gets up to in front you, try not to react in any way because it will just encourage him. You'll feel a mild burning sensation on your neck but that means it's working. Remember, no talking, no eating, no drinking and no laughing."

I nod gravely at her because Sally doesn't seem like the type of lady you ignore. Clive hands her the basket of kittens and after giving me one more stern look, she takes them and Snowbird away with her into a small backroom.

"Come on, my swiney princess," Clive says, giving me a deep bow and pointing at the doorway. "I'll take you to see Snuzzle."

Chapter Thirteen

As we're walking back down the hallway, and thankfully away from the room of chickens, I want to tell him not to call me that, but heed Sally's warning. So instead, I glare at him with pursed lips. A large and lazy smile spreads across his perfect face and his eyes go wide at my expression and he stops just outside the nearest lift.

"Oh, this is going to be fun," he teases, propping a hand on the wall above my head as he leans down to look at me and we wait for the lift to arrive. I haven't given his jacket back to him and it has left him in nothing but a thin white shirt, which I can't help but notice clings to his broad chest and really makes his muscles pop. What a clown would need with so much muscle, I don't know, but then I remember his past life as some sort of tumbler.

My face begins to flush thinking of what his muscular body could be capable of, but he takes it as a reaction to his teasing and the names become worse and worse.

"Let's see, Swiney Princess, Princess of Pigs, the Swiney Queen of Pigdom Country, The Countess of Pigs, The Pig Heiress..."

I feel the last name tangle inside my gut and I look away from him. I feel the color run from my cheeks and pool within my belly. He raises an eyebrow at my reaction and leans back, withdrawing his hand and placing both fists in the pockets of his pants. He rocks on his heels a few times before speaking again.

"Looks like I took that a little too far," he says softly, pulling out his hands and running a hand through his unruly, sandy hair. "How about I keep to calling you 'Bluebell' and maybe 'Bluey' on special occasions, and if I ever cross the line again, I'll owe you a kitten."

I smile at him and he gives me an easy grin in return as I nod in agreement. Though I can't help but roll my eyes at him.

"Or maybe we can take it one step further and I'll owe you a date or something," he adds, giving me a bold wink as the lift door finally opens for us.

Clive is utterly and devastatingly attractive, but I just don't know if I can think about that right now. Maybe later, but not until I'm able to sort out the rest of my life. All I can do now is blush in response to his flirting and turn away so he can't see the redness in my cheeks. Luckily we've arrived in a bigger lift and I can put a little distance between us as the lift bumps us along until it stops and we walk out into a long mahogany hallway.

It feels as if we've emerged into an entirely different reality as soon as the lift doors open and Clive and I step into what he calls the 'Staging Area,' or at least the part of the train where most of the Stage Girls live.

Some kind of smell laced with sugar and perfume floats by us and practically carries Clive away from me before he remembers me and grabs a hold of my hand. The familiarity of the gesture reminds me too much of Milo and I pull away, but give him a warm smile instead. I don't want him to think I'm not somewhat interested in him, even if he is a weird, cat-obsessed clown.

"What smells so good?" Clive leans in close and asks. "That's what you're thinking, right?" I give him a nod as he gestures for me to follow him and says over his shoulder, "Someone is always eating something around here. It's probably cake."

There is so much going on around me that it's hard to take it all in. Doors line the sides of the hall and we occasionally pass by one that is open. Inside I see large, floor to ceiling windows that show the landscape flashing by in a dizzying blur. The carpet beneath us is a deep, burgundy red and while it isn't plush by any means, it looks and feels relatively smooth and unblemished. Above our heads are lines strung from one side to the other and they hang with various dripping laundry from shirts and pants to a few dozen bras that Clive pretends to ignore, even when one of them falls off and onto his shoulders.

Amid this colorful chaos is an even more colorful assortment of people moving back and forth between rooms, calling to each other and laughing and talking and swinging and swearing up a storm for what seems like no particular reason.

"Always the liveliest part of the train," Clive tells me, leading me through a collection of women and a few men until we arrive at one of the open rooms. "The cats like a quieter existence so I'm shacked up a few floors down. They are doing construction on the other half of this floor, making new rooms and all that. It's been sealed off since they busted out all the windows, so everyone is packed tightly in here."

I nod, but can barely focus on him because so many other things demand my attention. I'm reminded of the cold, dark hallways of my family's estate and how the only sounds were the echoing footsteps of the mansion's staff or the far distance screaming of

Mary as she ran through the gardens. Even the bookshop with Flame held a more serene and noiseless life.

And while my past is completely different than what my senses are currently being assaulted with, the pit in my stomach begins to flutter as if it were full of butterflies and I can't help myself from throwing my arms around Clive's neck and giving him a hug, which he politely returns before gently pushing me away and pointing me into the open room before us.

"Don't want to be giving anyone a free showing." He laughs.

"Aww, but why ever not?" The high-pitched tune of Snuzzle drifts towards me and I nervously turn my attention from Clive's warm body to look into the room and come face to face with the first odd creature to come into my life.

"Hi," I croak and scratch absently at my neck. Snuzzle lets out a high-pitched sneeze in response. Clive gives me a look that tells me to stop itching myself and keep quiet before turning to Snuzzle.

"Neck trauma," he simply states, and even though I feel Snuzzle's assessing look on me, he doesn't question it.

"Ah, well, happens to the best of us," he finally says and claps his hands. He places one of those gold ornate fans that he was just using on the nearby table. I'm craning to look at the gorgeous motif of colorful swirls when Snuzzle clicks his tongue to get my attention. "Looks like you found a way to come with us after all. And you." He points to Clive. "Get out of here before you give me an asthmatic attack from all that cat hair I see on your clothes."

I give Snuzzle as wide of a smile as I can without feeling like my skin will rip apart, but he isn't paying attention while he blows his nose on a silk handkerchief.

"Ah, good, you two know each other." Clive laughs before bowing deeply to me. After he gives me a bold wink after rising back up he reaches for my hand. Before I can pull away, I realize he isn't going to kiss it, he merely places a small slip of paper into my palm.

"This is my room," he leans in and whispers. "Make sure to stop by and see the kittens." Then, after leaning away, he gives a dramatic wave to Snuzzle before exiting the room.

"Okay, let's see - ACHOO!" Snuzzle begins before having to back away from me and I remember I'm still wearing Clive's patchwork jacket.

I shrug my shoulders and take it off, folding it as tightly as possible and tucking it under my arm. Snuzzle is giving me a weary look as he returns to the opposite side of the room, but a pounding at his open door makes us both turn.

"You made it!" a girl screams and I find Minty standing here, then with much more grace than I would think her leg would make her capable of, she comes over and wraps me in a warm embrace.

"Just barely," I croak and she steps back to examine my neck. "I had to sneak onboard with Rose's help, but I think she may have left me for dead."

Frowning deeply, Minty gives me a sad look and crosses her arms against her chest. "The world can be unfair and cruel sometimes," she says and I hear Snuzzle grunt in agreement. He hasn't come near me again, probably keeping his distance in case I have more car fur hidden on my body, but he's made himself busy looking through a large trunk in the corner of his room. Both Minty and I look over with interest.

He's pulling out all sorts of garments and placing them in neat piles on the ground and I can't help but admire the elegant rainbow of fabrics that soon decorate his entire room. He may be searching deep for something within that trunk of his, but in my eyes, he's already unearthed a rainbow from seemingly nowhere.

It almost matches the shirt he's chosen to wear today, which itself is a rainbow of colors. Minty is dressed simply, just a shift dress in a thick pink fabric. There is a hint of shimmer within the threads and I wonder if the dress may have started life out as something different, but found new life in its current form and owner. My fingers itch to feel it and maybe make an alteration or two so that it fits her frame in a more flattering way, but Snuzzle distracts me from my thoughts when he holds up a pair of thick, yellow socks and a small booklet.

"These are for you," he says, handing them both to me. Minty coos in admiration at the socks.

"Um, thank you?" I tell him and tuck the strange gifts under my arm with Clive's jacket.

"Now, the question is where will I put you? Seeing as you're..." Snuzzle drifts off in thought but Minty springs to action before he can even finish his thought.

"We have an extra bed!" she yells. "She can stay with Butterscotch and me."

Snuzzle shrugs and lets out another sneeze.

"Fine, great, just get her out of here and show her where the showers are located." He points a finger at me. "Don't wear that coat around me again."

Minty laughs and I don't know whether I should take him seriously or not, but she begins dragging me out into the hallway and all I can give him is a nod and a smile before he disappears from view.

"Those are some nice socks," Minty tells me and the honesty on her face is so endearing that I have to laugh. She smiles brightly in return and pulls me further down the lines of open and closed doors. "Oh, and keep the booklet with you," she adds.

It seems to get louder and more chaotic the further down the hallway we travel, but Minty doesn't seem to pay any attention to it.

"Does anyone get any sleep around here?" I ask her after we pass by one of the rooms so tightly packed with people that they were spilling out into the hallway. They all looked really happy as they passed drinks and slices of cake to each other as we passed, but were also very loud. My palms were beginning to sweat from having to squeeze through so many loud bodies, but we luckily passed them quickly.

"Don't worry, it's not always this bad. I think someone had a birthday or something. Those days tend to get rowdy, but everyone here does have such different schedules and sleeping habits, so someone is always awake." She shrugs and gestures about. "But it gives this place a homely vibe in my opinion. So many of the girls here lacked that growing up, I think, so we kind of made our own family here."

Her comments make me pause mid-step and think about the concept of found family. I was never particularly close to the people who brought me into this world. Patrick was always two steps ahead of me in the maturity department and we never got along, and Mary was too young for me to form any real kind of friendship. Belle wasn't around long enough for me to get to know her before she died.

I guess that leaves Milo and Flame, and while I still don't want to think too much about Milo, Flame was probably the only real family I had growing up. I wonder how she's doing and if they questioned her about my disappearance. I'll need to write to her very soon.

Minty stopped talking and I could tell she was being polite and giving me a chance to think about everything. I shift on my feet and scratch idly at my neck.

"Thank you," I whisper and I'm glad she can even hear me. Sally mentioned I needed to keep quiet while my neck was healing, but she didn't mention that I wouldn't have much of a choice in the matter.

Minty beams at me anyway and points at one of the closed doors.

"Problem with being one of the last recruits is that you don't get much of a say where you end up, but you could do worse than bunking with Butter and me. She keeps to herself and sleeps most of the day anyway," she says, pushing the door open with her foot.

We step inside a small, rectangular room that stretches out in front of me and ends in one of the large floor to ceiling windows. Along one side is a small bed with a pile of clothes stacked haphazardly on top, no more of a cot, and another runs parallel on the opposite wall. Minty lets me go inside first and then she follows me, closing the door behind her. Someone has turned down all the lights and I watch as she flips them on using a small side panel.

"Wake up Butter! We have a new roomie!"

The pile of blankets shifts around and I jump back in surprise as the bed ragged head of a small girl pokes out and looks at us through squinted eyes. She looks young, almost too young to be required to start her Required Service, but I hold my tongue. There are many young people who are desperate enough to fudge the paperwork, especially if they need a way out of something and I can't judge anyone for that. And the last thing I need is to speak my mind and get myself in trouble with my new roommates.

"Wha?" she says in a raspy voice and Minty giggles as Butterscotch rubs her eyes.

"Long night on the dining floor?"

"Like you wouldn't believe," she wails, burrowing back under the pile of blankets and clothing. Minty pats the pile where I assume her head would be.

"Working the dining floor is the worst, people are so messy and you don't get to eat any food until the end of your shift and then all the good stuff is gone!"

I smile in reply, not ready to think about what actually working will be like, and walk towards the big window. I'm mesmerized by the land speeding past us outside and the far, far below us and have to back away.

"How far up are we?" I rasp out and Minty comes to stand by my side.

"You don't really want to know," she whispers.

"It's best not to think about it," says the pile of clothes behind us and Minty laughs fully and loudly.

And in that moment, her laugh reminds me of Flame and this cozy but small room is the bookshop. There is even a pile of books off to my side that could belong right in that little place I left behind with the rest of my life. The terrain outside begins to make me dizzy so I turn fully around and face Minty, who has just pulled down what looks like a third cot that hovers in the middle of the wall above Butterscotch's bed.

And while a part of my heart still hurts for the easy but controlled life I left behind in Pioneer Springs, I find that for the first time in a long while, I'm excited for what the future will bring.

Chapter Fourteen

"I don't know about you guys, but I need something to eat," Minty says suddenly and laughs at the bright reaction I must have on my face. "Well, looks like Bluebell is hungry. Butter? You want to get an early dinner?"

"Nope," she mutters, burrowing deeper into her blankets.

"I am really hungry," I manage to say. The words seem to come out a little easier and I marvel at whatever Sally put on my neck. And while I remember how she warned about having a nasty scar afterward, I'd gladly bear that for a grilled cheese and some tomato soup right now.

I fold up the socks from Snuzzle and place them delicately on my new bed. They are all I currently have left to my name right now and I might as well take good care of them. However, I don't take off the patchwork jacket because I can tell by the darkening sky outside our window that it may be cold tonight.

Then I remember there is one more thing I have: the engagement ring. When neither of the girls is looking, I check my pocket to make sure it's still tucked inside, but I don't take it out. It's too valuable to leave behind, and I feel like I should keep it on me.

"I have diner floor duty tonight," Minty informs us, as she pulls out a jacket of her own. It's cropped vegan leather and sits just above her hips and I can't help but reach out and finger the fine sticking.

"This is super cute!"

"Thank you! I got it at that shop you showed to us. Well, technically Snuzzle got it, I just, um, took it from him. It's okay, though, I think he got it for me anyway or at least it looks better on me than him."

I smile and let the fabric go, not really wanting to think about Theo's Threadshop anymore than I have to, but Minty is already heading out the door and I quickly move to follow.

"You'll get your proper assignments tomorrow or maybe the next day. We're due in Searless tomorrow, I think. Actually I'm not sure, but I know there's a show happening tomorrow. Might as well come with me tonight so I can show you what it's like."

I nod along with her comments and continue following her down the hall. We pass by at least one more party, but more doors seem to be closed on this end of the hall. Minty tells me everyone is probably sleeping from having to get up early for morning duties. She says they sometimes have to wake up at dawn, depending on what their assignments are and I turn my head away so she doesn't see the color drain from my face at the thought of waking up that early.

"Afterwards, I'll take you by costume and general storage. We can find you some things to wear." She pauses now and stops so suddenly in her tracks that I bump into her. It causes her to sway on her bad leg and I reach out to help steady her. She smiles nervously and looks at me when she's back on two feet. "I, um, don't want to pry. It's not the circus way. No one ever asks and fewer people even consider telling, but if you ever need to talk about how you ended up here with that injury and nothing but the clothes on your back, I'll be here to listen."

I smile at her sincere gesture, but wave her off. "It's actually fairly simple. I ran away from an awful arranged marriage, was chased by my family and jumped on the train just as it was leaving the station."

"You're married?"

"Nope, ran away ten minutes before the ceremony."

Minty's eyes go wide. "And your family chased you?"

"Well, actually it was someone who works for my family."

I leave out mentioning anything about Robbie and Milo, but if Minty's eyes could get any wider, I think they would. But instead of prying, she clasps her hands to her chest and sighs dreamily.

"This sounds straight out of a romance novel!" She gives a practiced twirl that I'm surprised she manages with her injured leg.

"You sound like my friend, Flame," I blurt out and feel the tug of pain in my stomach at her memory, but Minty laughs loudly and it brings me back into the moment.

"The girl at the bookshop? She was a kindred spirit when it came to romantic tales."

"She was really into them," I say and can't help the sigh that escapes my mouth. "I miss her."

Minty takes my hands.

"I can't replace your missing friend, but I'll do my best to help keep her place warm in your heart."

"Now you sound as if you're coming right out of a romance novel," I tell her and she squeals in delight.

"Let's get going, or we won't get a chance to eat before the dinner rush comes in," she says brightly and continues down the hall. I follow behind her and my steps feel just a little lighter as we make our way to the closest lift. It feels good to admit out loud that I finally took my life into my own hands.

It's a nice feeling, but I wonder if I should be honest with her and tell her I plan on making a run for it at some point, that I'm not sure even the circus can keep me safe. Robbie and Patrick have no doubt figured out by now that it was my only way out of town and what if they're already waiting for me when we stop in Searless?

My dark thoughts are dispersed when the lift doors open smoothly as we arrive in from of them and a tall man walks out. His dark green eyes scan over our faces and he quickens his pace without a word to either of us, but I can't help but stare after his wake and ask Minty who he was.

"One of our top performers named Jack," she whispers when he's much, much further down the hallway. She then snickers loudly. "I don't think he likes coming down here often because every boy and girl gushes over him. But maybe he's looking for Clive's mystery cat, rumor says he's offering a reward to whoever finds him."

"Hmm, I mean he's cute, but looks like the kind that gets stuck in their own thoughts," I mutter. He's far enough away not to hear us though and true to Minty's words, a group of girls have emerged from one of the doorways and are attempting to follow him. He's attractive but I don't like the swagger to his movements, they don't look as easygoing as Clive. "I like them a little more down to earth."

"Like Kitty Cat Clive?" Minty asks in a sing-song voice almost as if she could read my thoughts and I feel my cheeks heat up as she bats her eyes at me and giggles.

"Maybe," I mumble as we step into the waiting lift.

"He's an odd one, loves his cats more than anyone else I hear, but you could do worse I guess."

Flashes of Robbie Lester come pouring into my head and even Milo's kind but distant voice glides over my memory. How long will it be until I stop thinking about either of them? I give Minty a vigorous nod because she's right, I could do worse. Like pining after someone who apparently never had these kinds of feelings for me or being stuck in an aggressive and unpredictable marriage. The ring in my pocket burns in agreement.

"Well, maybe we'll run into him tonight at work," Minty says encouragingly and I try to laugh her off. I don't have time for Clive right now, I need to get my life in this new place sorted out first. At least that is what I'm going to keep telling myself.

"Something smells really good." An alluring smell begins wafting out my direction the second the lift doors open and I'm distracted from my thoughts. My stomach rumbles greedily and I think about how long it's been since I've had anything more than water.

"Did you remember to bring the book Snuzzle gave you?" Minty asks and I give her a distracted nod. "Good, you'll need that to get food."

She then grabs my hand and pulls me inside a room with more people inside than I think live in the town of Pioneer Springs.

The lift lets us out onto an expansive floor that has been densely packed with a wash of different tables and chairs. There are buffet

stations set up along each of the walls and while one side looks as if it's been closed off, the other is packed with simmering trays and bowls of food.

I follow my nose and wander to the closest one that has three big bowls set upon it, each with a different colored rice dish. Minty follows and stands behind me as she points out different dishes and gives her brutally honest opinion on each one. But to be fair, I don't think my stomach can afford to be picky right now.

Still, there is a small amount of my upbringing that I've never been quite able to shake off: table manners.

I take a moment to settle myself before carefully spooning a moderate portion of the greenest rice onto a plate. Minty commends my choice but warns me that it'll make my breath 'stink all the way up to the heavenly starlings,' which she tells me is slang that she picked up on even though she has no idea what it means.

After she serves herself a pile of brown rice studded with black beans, we move down the line and I come to face with a tower of bread rolls. I take one large fluffy biscuit-looking one and a dollop of pink colored butter, which Minty tells me is plant-based and flavored like raspberries.

"Does the circus ever serve meat in here?" I ask out of curiosity.

"Not really, did you want some?" Minty asks.

"No! I mean, no thank you. I actually don't eat any meat products," I tell her and she nods in understanding.

"We occasionally get a shipment or two that we pick up during our stopovers and it's typically a big hit with maybe about half the people here. But it's expensive stuff and, well, between you and me, I just feel so guilty about it. I mean, isn't meat eating what created the Dusting? Maybe we shouldn't be eating stuff like that."

"I couldn't agree more."

"Oh good, this is why we're going to be such good friends," she says with a beaming smile that quickly drops as she glances over my shoulder at something that has caught her attention. She looks straight at me and whispers, "Don't look. It's Rose and I think she may be coming over."

I do the exact opposite and turn to glare at the incoming girl. She looks better now, more rested and she's dabbed on quite a bit of makeup to cover the bruising I remember seeing on her face. And at least she has the decency to look ashamed when she notices me, though I have trouble believing there is any sincerity in her expression.

"I'm so glad you're okay," she says, drawing out her words in a way that makes my skin crawl. "I went to check on you and couldn't find you. I feared you may have fallen off the train or something."

Minty flicks a stray black bean at Rose and scowls. "You probably left her for dead."

"Is that what she told you?" Rose says and the sneer she gives us is utterly disgusting and makes me want to slap her. But once again, I remember my table manners and try a different tactic.

"Well, you held up your end of the deal, you helped me get here, so I guess I can't be too upset," I say between gritted teeth. I make to turn around and put it behind me, but remember something else and add, "By the way, can I get my scarf back?"

Rose looks up from picking at her nails.

"I thought you wouldn't mind if I kept it, it is such a pretty thing."

"Actually, I do mind. It belonged to my friend," I tell her and Rose laughs.

"Give it back to her," says Minty, shifting to stand by my side. Rose eyes her up and down, lingering on her bad leg a tad longer than necessary before rolling her eyes at both of us.

"If it belonged to her friend to begin with then I don't see why it matters so much," she says. "It doesn't belong to her."

"It doesn't belong to you either and besides, I made it so you could say that it was mine to begin with after all."

"There's no way you made that thing, it's too artistic and from what I heard about you in your... quaint little town of Pioneer Springs, is that you're a spoiled little heiress to a pig farm." She gives a mighty laugh and moves off to join another group of girls and women sitting at a nearby table. Most of them laugh along with her, but more than a few look embarrassed and change tables.

"Come on, we'll get this sorted later," says Minty. "We don't have much time to eat before shift change."

I sigh as loudly and dramatically as I possibly can and follow her to a short man who grabs our little books and embosses them with a quick stamp before shooing us away. We then make our way to an empty table towards the back of the giant room. Minty leaves me for a moment to get us a couple glasses of water and while she's gone, my gaze shifts out a nearby window. It looks like we're traveling north because to our side is a brilliant orange and gold sunset.

I also noticed the air looks cleaner and clearer than I've seen in a while. There was always such a haze to everything at home since we were so close to the Dustings, as if everything was covered with an opaque film that blurred the sharp edges of everything and everyone.

But out here, everything is in focus.

"Mind if I join you?" the deep rumbling voice of Clive pops me back into the present and I move over to make room for him to sit down.

"Sorry, just a little lost in thought," I say and he shrugs with an easy roll back of his shoulders.

"No worries at all, think away. Besides, I'm used to people ignoring me."

"By people, I'm assuming you mean your cats," Minty informs him, sitting down to join us.

"Why do you ask? Did you see the black and white cat?" Clive asks hopefully but Minty waves her fork at him.

"Well, if he doesn't show himself, the government will be after him for not signing for up his Required Service!"

Clive and Minty fall into laughter and it's too contagious not to get caught up in their fun. And then in-between jokes, centered mostly on stories of Clive's cats getting into mischief with the circus clowns, I finish my plate of rice in record time and even part of Minty's brown portion with beans that she offers to me. I've just polished off the last delicious bite of my biscuit dripping in melty raspberry butter when a dark shadow descends upon our table.

"I had an idea," says Rose, leaning forward and placing her palms on the table in front of me. I turn in my seat to look up at her and scowl.

"An idea?" Clive asks for me.

"Yup, I was talking with the girls and they too were admiring your friend's fancy scarf. You said you made it?"

I nod, unclear of where she's headed with this conversation. I can feel Minty tapping her foot under the table in annoyance and Clive's posture has stiffened beside me. It's unclear how much better they know Rose than I do, but from what I've experienced, she's no better than rancid hog fat.

"Perfect, then how about this. I don't really believe someone like you." She pauses to assess me with a critical eye before she goes on. "I don't think someone like you could actually be capable of hard, creative work. You know, the kind that it takes to work some place like here? So, I wager that you won't be able to find and convince a troupe of performers here to wear something you've created to the performance tomorrow."

"Why on earth would I take you up on something like that? There are no stakes at all and barely any time to make something," I tell her and begin to turn away, but before I can, she's bending forward to get in my face.

"I'll give your scarf back to you and if you can't, then I get to keep it or maybe I'll pop it in the smoke stacks and watch it burn." She smiles wide but it doesn't reach her eyes and there is a cold and wicked humor in her fair features as if she's very much enjoying being mean. "It's obvious you want it back, I can see it on your face."

I shift in my seat and pull away from her just as Clive stands up behind me and faces her down. There is a tense moment between the two of them, but Rose backs away first.

"So, do we have a deal? Or would you rather we play for that pretty ring I know you have stored in your pocket?" she asks and before she can say anything else, I hold my hand out for her to shake. She eyes it, as if it could be some sort of trap, but takes it anyway. I give her the two ups and downs of a Florence family handshake and turn back to my almost empty plate of food.

I can hear Rose laughing as she walks away and Clive lowers himself back into his seat beside me. Minty is chewing her lip and looks nervous. I raise an eyebrow at her.

"What ring?" Clive asks.

"It's nothing," I say, fighting the warming flush creeping over my skin.

Minty notices my discomfort and possibly the way my hand clenches against my pocket, and she clears her throat to draw Clive's attention to her.

"Well," she says slowly, spinning her fork around her now empty plate. "Rose trapped you on that one because there's no way you'll be able to accomplish something like that at this hour. Not the night before a performance. Unless you're some sort of miracle worker with a lot of secret connections to the troupe leads that I don't know about, I think she tricked you good. Why would you even agree to something like that?"

Chapter Fifteen

A pit forms in my stomach and I look up from our table and glance at Rose, who is now standing and collecting her friends to leave the dining floor. Minty is right, I got caught up in the moment and wasn't thinking straight. I can't quite understand why Rose has it out for me, but I let her get to me and now I may regret it. I know it's just a silly scarf, but after losing everything at the train station, it's the only remembrance I have of my past life.

"I'm not sure... I don't think I've ever come across a person like that," I mutter, turning back and facing Minty and Clive. "Actually, I take that back, I know a guy that would be perfect for her. She just got to me, I think."

Clive raises an eyebrow and Minty sighs.

"She's been here longer than I have, but I don't think she likes it. I told you about the rumor that she gets off at every stop to look for some rich single man or woman to take her in, you know, to trap into a marriage."

"No one should ever be trapped," I find myself saying. I'm glad I ate all my food before speaking with Rose because the way my stomach pinches together makes me feel sick. Clive puts a reassuring hand on my shoulder before getting up from the table and stretching.

"I have an idea," he says. Minty and I look at him and he gives us an easy smile and takes his time smoothing out his shirt.

"Well, what is it?" asks Minty.

"Don't know yet, but I'll catch you after work. I should know by then," he says and gives me a wink before walking off towards a group of clowns just leaving through the closest lift.

"He is so strange," I say to Minty once he's gone and she nods vigorously before stacking our dishes together.

"At least he's got his looks going for him," she says with a shrug. "Come on, let's get to work."

"Right now?" I blurt out, looking around the room that is rapidly emptying of people.

"Afraid so." She sighs and hands me our dishes. One of my fingers presses into a lone black bean on her plate and it squishes inside the under part of my nail. I fight the urge to drop the plate.

"Um, what exactly are we doing?" I ask.

"Cleaning everything."

"Everything?"

"Everything."

What follows is probably the most work I have ever had to do in my entire life. It makes me think of all the meals served to me inside my family's estate. Just how many dishes did I manage to dirty and who exactly cleaned them? It sure wasn't me and I have to say as much to Minty when I follow her back, loaded with stacks of half-empty plates of food that I'm barely able to see over.

We end up in a room nearly as large as the dining floor but covered in stoves, ovens, fryers and sinks. Minty points me towards a tall sink and I line up next to another girl with thick brown hair. It's too loud to hear anything back here with the sounds of pouring water and dishes being dropped into the bubbling sinks, but the girl gestures at the plates and I begin to hand them to her one by one while she cleans and dries each one.

Then to my dismay, she leaves and pushes me into her space and I find myself in front of the sink. I have the wit to roll up the sleeves of Clive's jacket, but there's little protection from the scalding temperature and gooey, mushy feeling of wet food as it slides off the plates and into mechanized disposals set deep within the drains.

It takes a few minutes, but I finally get into a good pattern of rinsing and repeating, as well as gagging and cringing, and in between scrubbing hardened cheeses and scraping off dried up gravies, I start to feel different. A real appreciation settles over me for what goes on in the kitchen that doesn't involve the eating of food.

BUT.

That doesn't mean I have to like it. It's in fact, very disgusting and I feel like the skin on my hands may be melted off from the hot water and been replaced with gloopy, wet food.

"I'm so tired," I complain to Minty and another girl whose name I didn't hear over the sounds of rushing water and clanging dishes.

"You get used to it," the unknown girl says and offers me a stick of gum to chew. "Just try to zone out and focus on what you're doing, not what you're thinking of it."

"Oh, I'm thinking of so many things right now," I grumble and wipe the sweat from my forehead.

"Luckily, this is one of the harder jobs around here." Minty laughs and the other girl nods.

"Yeah, this is gross, but working concessions and helping out with the actual shows is why most people sign up to work here."

"Well, they certainly can't advertise this mess," I say. "No one would ever join up."

"Is it not the glamorous lifestyle you're used to?" a plain looking girl with long brown hair asks a few sinks down from us. I recognize her as one of the girls sitting earlier with Rose.

"You're so right," I snip back at her. "I keep waiting for the butlers to come by and bring some lotion for my hands, but none have arrived yet. Such a pity, looks like I'll have to retire to my velvet covered bed beneath my crystal chandelier with chapped skin. What a travesty!"

Minty snickers as the brown-haired girl rolls her eyes and switches places with someone else. She then elbows me hard in my ribs and points to one of the doorways.

"Looks like you have a visitor," she says and waggles her eyebrows at me. The unknown girl looks over as well and laughs brightly.

"Oh, it's Kitty Cat Clive!"

Clive, upon seeing us and hearing his name, swaggers over with all the grace of the jungle documentary leopards I used to watch with Milo when we were kids. I guess his nickname is well deserved, he is rather cat-like.

"And how is the working life suiting you?" He comes up to us and asks me with a wide grin. I notice out of the corner of my eye that Minty and the other girl have moved off to the side and are pretending not to pay attention.

"Well," I start, wiping my hands across my forehead one more time and trying to smooth my hair which has become frizzled by the humid kitchen hair. "It's not as bad as I thought it'd be."

"Hmm," Clive trills as he considers me. His eyes roam my body in a way that feels like he's sizing me up as a cat would do to its prey and I can't tell if I like it or feel overly exposed. But I don't have time to dwell on the feeling before Minty jumps into our conversation.

"Looks like that's the last of it," she says and I look down at my sink to find it surprisingly empty. The conversation and company must have made time move that much quicker.

"Perfect," says Clive. "I was doing some thinking and checking and I came up with a solution to your problem from earlier."

"And what would that be?" I ask, stepping away from the still warm sink and looking up at him. He gives me a feral grin.

"Rose said you have to find a performing troupe and it just so happens that I'm in charge of one."

Minty has come over now and I can see her bouncing on her heels in laughter because she's caught onto something that hasn't hit me just yet.

"You are?" I ask, folding my arms across my chest and trying to ignore Minty's giggling. "I didn't know that. I mean, I figured you performed with the clowns, but wasn't sure how exactly that worked."

"Yup, I'm in charge of five separate performers, sometimes six if Trixie is feeling up to performing or not, and I decide on what they wear and what they do."

It takes longer than I'd like to admit to come to the conclusion about what Clive is talking about, but when it hits me, I can't help but slap a palm over my face.

"You're talking about your cats, aren't you?" I ask and he smacks me on the back as if we were old friends.

"You bet your little piggy butt I am!"

"Okay, first off, 'little piggy butt?' Ew, no. And second, would that even count?"

Minty shrugs in response and gestures for me to follow her out of the kitchen. I didn't notice before, but as we'd been talking, a whole group of new people had been pouring into the room and she told me it was the dinner cooks. Clive saunters to the same lift I saw him use earlier and presses a button to call it, but Minty hangs back.

"As much as I would love to come, I'm really more of a dog person. I'll pick you up some clothes and stuff from storage and leave it on your bed. Can you find your way back to the room?" she asks me, but Clive answers instead.

"I'll walk her back afterward and promise to have her home before midnight," he says, which makes Minty giggle all the more as she skips away.

I turn to Clive, unable to keep from blushing as he looks back at me. If he had been born in Pioneer Springs, every girl in that city would be in love with him, myself included. I thought Milo was cute, but wow, the way Clive's chiseled features and deep blue eyes make him look both rugged and soft at the same time makes my head spin.

"Lost in thought?" he asks and I snap myself back to the present.

"I was just thinking of how I could make outfits for cats," I lie.

"Don't think about it too much because I can promise you that no matter how much you think about doing something like that, actually doing it is much, much harder. Trust me, I've tried."

I'm about to ask for more information, but the lift doors open before us and we step inside one of the smaller lifts that puts us almost right up against each other.

I can feel my heart beating and I wonder why I'm so nervous. Maybe it's just fatigue. I mean, it's barely been a day or two since I was last in Pioneer Springs and while that place feels like a million miles and years away, the pain it left in my soul is still fresh and I want to protect my new life as much as possible.

Still, the way Clive's own chest moves up and down under that thin white shirt is distracting and I find my gaze moving to his arms, his neck and eventually eyeing his perfectly shaped mouth to wonder if kissing him would be like kissing Milo last summer.

But luckily the lift door hisses open and distracts me from my utterly dangerous thoughts and I follow Clive out into a place completely different than the Stage Girls area in almost every way imaginable.

The long hallway still has the shining mahogany wood but it seems to glisten with a fresh shine that speaks of long-time care and maintenance. The carpet is plush and feels squishy under my feet and looks as if it's hardly ever been used or that someone takes very good care of it as well. The smell of crisp lemon and rosemary wafts towards us through a long line of closed doors, and I think that somewhere, someone is playing a violin.

"Wow, it's very, um, posh in here," I say and Clive gives me an exaggerated bow as he points down the hallway.

"Surprised?" he asks, head still pointed down at my feet and I have to laugh.

"I don't know, I've only seen the storage rooms, the food rooms and the rooms the Stage Girls call home and none of those places compare to this. This actually feels more like where I grew up, like home."

I say it before I really think about the word 'home' but as soon as it's out, the pit in my stomach is back. It's part remembrance and longing for those rare, good parts of my old life, but also a sickening reminder that fine places such as these can hide dark secrets.

Clive looks as if he notices my discomfort because he stands straight and cocks his head to the side as he looks at me.

"Do you want to talk about it? Or if not, do you want to leave?"

"Oh, no," I say, grateful for his sincere tone. "It's fine. It's just that this place looks a lot like the, um, house, I grew up in."

"I didn't know that houses in Pioneer Springs looked this grand."

"Well, most don't exactly, but mine was... different."

"Ah, I see. Well, I'm sure it was fit for an heiress as gentle and beautiful as yourself," he says with a wink and I can't hold in my laughter as he drops to a knee and pretends to grovel at my feet.

"You are embarrassing!" I snap, leaping back as he stands back up and laughs lightly.

"You know, people tell me that all the time? I think it's because they're just not used to my personal style of flattery. Trust me, I only grovel at the feet of those truly worthy of it," he says and leads me down the quiet hall towards the tinkling sound of music. The violin has stopped and someone has taken up the sad lullaby of an old song played on the piano. If I didn't know any better, I'd say Clive was escorting me to a grand ballroom in some even grander mansion.

"How would you know I'm worth anything?" I whisper, lost in thoughts of fine dresses, dark hallways and rich smelling air.

"It's easy, anyone who would cuddle with a mother cat and her kittens late into the night to help them keep warm is worth more than all the diamonds in the sky."

His words leave me speechless and I'm at a loss for a response, but he doesn't seem to care as he continues down the plush carpets and gestures for me to follow.

Chapter Sixteen

My slow footsteps are silent as I walk after Clive and I can't help taking my time down the enchanting hallway. I'm disappointed that none of the doors are open because I wonder if the individual rooms are as pristine as the smoothly polished hallway banister, I can't help but run my hands across.

Even the names above the doors are different and each is wooden and carved and old. I stop to admire one and Clive turns around to see what has caught my attention and smiles at me.

"Old family names," he explains. "Most people here can trace their circus roots back for generations. The older looking and more distinguished looking your name plaque generally means you're from a longer line and that you can trace your ancestors back to a time when there were lion tamers and performing giraffes."

"Is that true for your family?" I can't help but ask.

"Yes, but not around here." He gestures around the hall. "They took to the skies, but little Clive felt his calling from another direction."

"Hmm, I guess I can relate."

"Then I'm glad to know I'm in relatable company," he says, pausing at the last two doors in the long hallway. The furthest door, just next to the one we stand at now, is shut tight and has a warning sign posted neatly upon it. Written in a flowing script and framed in a gold-colored frame are the words, "Do not open, cats inside."

"Which door is your room?" I ask dryly. "Is it the cat one?"

"You'll see." He laughs, opening the other door and allowing me to enter first.

There is a great scattering noise that welcomes me and it sounds like tiny nails skittering along a crystal table top. It takes a moment for my eyes to adjust to the dim light, but before they fully can focus, Clive leans over and switches on a light beside the door.

"It's usually much brighter in here," he mutters, looking around. "Someone must have knocked over a lamp."

I step inside a room the exact same size as the one I'm currently sharing with Minty and Butterscotch, but it appears Clive has this entire place to himself. It is set up simply, just a regular-sized bed by the wall with a large cage set up next to it, and a big desk across from a closed door.

The only thing that really stands out is the several carpeted platforms secured to the giant window. They are vacant of all but two cats now, but I can only imagine how many at a time might be there at one time watching the countryside fly by as if they too were the birds I'm sure they'd love to go hunting for.

"Ah, Snowy," Clive hums, bending down to pet the pretty mother cat as she trots over to us. She advances by his outstretched hand and ignores him while she chooses to instead twirl around my legs.

"Looks like she has a new favorite," I tell Clive and he scratches the back of his neck in thought.

"I guess so." He eventually laughs and moves towards the door beside the desk and opens it. As soon as he does, a multitude of furry bodies shoot out from beneath his bed and rush into the room next door, the one behind the sign warning about cats.

"Have a seat, I just have to go feed them," he says sheepishly and points to the only chair available, a big plush armchair in front of the window.

After Clive moves away, I go over and sit down carefully, afraid I may squash a hidden cat, but am relieved when nothing under me moves. From the sounds of it, they are all crowded around him in the other room and are begging, screaming, at him for food.

His room faces a different side of the train than my own and I can see that night has quickly fallen across the dry and desert like landscape crawling by. For reasons I'm uncertain of, the train is moving slower now and I pretend it's savoring the gorgeous sunset that slowly streaks along the sky ahead of us.

"Penny for your thoughts?" Clive says, coming over and taking a seat on the ground next to my knees. One of the cats has followed him over, a big fluffy black and white one, and it sits on his outstretched legs, purring in his lap. He leans back, pressing his palms against the floor and stares out at the sunset with me.

I don't feel like answering him right away and instead take the moment to relax to the sounds of the humming train around us and the soft vibrations of the fluffy cat.

"Sunsets back home were never like this," I finally say and he nods slowly.

"I always thought that the quality of a sunset is determined by whom it is shared with," says Clive and I fight the creeping blush spreading up my neck. I bring my legs up to tuck underneath me and twist in the chair so I'm facing him.

"A cat lover and a poet? You don't seem real," I tell him and he laughs, not making eye contact with me until he's done and when his darkly blue eyes do hit home, I have to turn away. I don't remember the last time I've been alone with anyone besides Milo, and even then, we were only ever truly alone one time and that's when things... ended poorly.

"I guess I am a catch," Clive sings suddenly and holds up the fluffy cat to me, pressing him into my chest. "But so is this one."

The cat does a very un-cat like thing and doesn't struggle to get away. Instead, he flops over on top of me and rolls over to expose his big belly. I tentatively rub it a few times, leery because I know how cats are, but the giant thing just purrs and accepts the pets as if we've known each other our whole lives. Much like his owner, Clive, I realize.

"This is Bruno," says Clive. "He's one of my top performers, well, when he wants to be and I have treats involved. I was thinking you could make him, oh I don't know... a hat. I think that would count for your little bet, right?"

I hold Bruno up and he lets his arms and legs hang lumpy while studying me with unearthly large, yellow eyes. His purring stops and we hold our eye connection for much longer than I am comfortable with, seeing he's a cat and trying to look into my soul. Which I don't think he can do... can he?

"Well, Bruno, let's see what we can do."

Clive has a friend from down the hall bring over a sewing machine and a huge box of scrap fabric. I ask the friend, who is a tall gangly man with a mustache grown so long that it curves around his ears, where the fabric came from and he waves a hand in a vague and dramatic circle above my head. A few speckles of glitter fall from his fingers and into my eyes.

"A magician never reveals his secrets, my dear, not even to circus folk," he says before disappearing out the door.

"Well, okay then," I tell the door and Clive chuckles.

"Sorry, everyone here is a little eccentric, especially the ones who take their jobs seriously, like Joel, who you just met. The fabric is probably left over from everyone's costumes and we share the sewing machine so it gets passed around from room to room. The clowns and I guess magicians if there are any in residence, make our own clothing because it's generally full of secrets."

"Makes sense," I mutter, sorting through the large tub of brightly colored fabrics, which I find to be absolutely and utterly perfect.

Clive leans in as I sort out several pieces in a shimming gold fabric and I can feel his warm breath on the back of my neck. It gives me a chill that travels from my toes to my own neck and I desperately hope he doesn't notice the goosebumps he's giving me for being this close.

I lean away, but he turns at the same time so that his nose bumps into the side of my cheek. Ducking away so he can't see my reaction, I hold the cloth up to Bruno, who lays patiently on his side by us.

"Do you think this will work?" I finally look over to ask Clive, but he's already staring at me and he visually swallows before looking down at the cat, back at me, to the cat again and then back to me.

"Perfect," he finally says, giving me a smile that makes me squirm just a little before I force the fun and flirty thoughts away from my mind. I have a job to do and it needs to get done soon. It's already getting very late into the night. Besides, I have no real way of knowing if the attraction goes both ways. I learned that the hard way from Milo, and I don't think I could handle another rejection like that.

Clive helps me hold Bruno still as I begin my work, which is quite a feat considering the gigantic cat has decided he'd much rather be anywhere else than near the sewing machine. From the corner of my eyes, I can see the mother cat, Snowbird, watching us and her squinting eyes give the impression that she's laughing at Bruno's misfortunate.

Don't worry, Snowy, you'll be next.

After some time, I'm able to contrast a glittering gold vest for Bruno that gives him the use of all four legs while still giving the impression of a tiny gold tuxedo.

"What a perfect little gentleman," coos Clive, letting him go. I watch as both Bruno and the glittering gold fabric disappear under the bed. I lean down to glance at him and his big round eyes look at me from the dark as if I betrayed both him and his ancestors going back thousands of years. Clive laughs as he makes his way into the second room and I stand to follow him.

It's another room exactly like all the other accommodations on the trains, except this one is dedicated to nothing but cats. Some litter pans line one wall and the other is covered in velvety cushions and wooden perches, some with dangling cat toys. I bop one of them with a finger and a slender all black cat with bright green eyes darts out and takes a similar swat before noticing me. She then very carefully reaches out her little face and sniffs my hand.

"Ah, perfect, this is Michelle. Bruno's partner, and she'll need her own matching dress," says Clive, pointing at her.

I take a chance and reach to pick her up, realizing I haven't handled cats this much since I was a child running around Swiney Acres.

"I forgot how much I like cats," I tell Clive just as Michelle crawls into my arms. "I used to play with the barn cats we had around my family's factories growing up and there were a few around the estate yards, but I noticed them less and less when I began hanging out in town more."

Clive lifts an eyebrow at me as we settle back down beside the sewing machine. Michelle, unlike her partner, sits like a perfect statue in front of me as I hold up pieces of fabric to her shiny black fur.

"So, you really are a Pig Heiress," Clive says softly and I turn to give him a hard look but find him smiling. So instead, I sigh so loudly that Michelle rubs her face against my cheek as if she can sense my discomfort. It forces a light laugh to escape and I rub her chin. She leans in closely as I speak softly to Clive.

"The Florence family owns Swiney Acres, the biggest pork supplier around. My oldest brother, Patrick, is set to inherit the place after my parents. My oldest sister, Belle, was supposed to marry into another wealthy family owning the biggest chicken farm. You know, to combine empires or some such nonsense."

"Did she?"

"She couldn't because she died." The words have trouble coming out, but I force them to anyway. "It was the year I was born, so I never knew her, and she was only ten years old."

"What happened?" Clive asks. I turn to him, but his focus is on Michelle as she purrs against my hand.

"No one knows," I say, the words drifting from me as if by speaking them aloud, the misery may somehow reveal itself. "She was playing with Robbie Lester, the oldest son of the nearby chicken empire and the guy she was supposed to marry one day, when he came running in saying she drowned in one of the garden pools."

The memory still brings the hairs on the back of my neck on end, even though I wasn't old enough to experience the moment firsthand, hearing the story from Milo one day gave me nightmares for weeks. It's not like he was old enough either, but his parents, unlike my own, didn't attempt to hide such dark secrets from his world.

"They tore down the gardens and filled in all the pools, now the grounds are nothing but smooth stone and statues made to resemble trees. I think she may be buried somewhere inside, but I never had enough courage to search for her headstone. They made me take her place and said I had to marry Robbie."

I can't help the shuddering sigh that comes out and Clive reaches to grab my hands, which I find shaking from nearly being lost in the memory. He brings them to his mouth and breathes on them and his breath is warm and hot and human and makes me smile.

"There, it looked like someone needed to breathe a little lightness into your heart," he tells me. "You're safe here."

I feel the pinching return to my stomach, but it's not from anxiety this time, it's from the way his eyes hood over when he looks at me and how we're sitting so close that our knees are pressed together.

I clear my throat and blush.

"We should get these costumes done before midnight or else Minty will come looking for us," I whisper and he leans back, smiling easily. He nods in agreement and rises on what appear to be shaking legs. Maybe he is just as distracted by me as I am with him. But what would I know? I read Milo's actions incorrectly for years. Clive is probably just trying to be nice.

"Agreed, why don't you continue on this and I'll go get us a snack," Clive says, jumping up and leaving so quickly that I can't even reply or get through another thought.

Michelle watches him go and swishes her tail a few times.

"I know," I coo to her. "Kitty Cat Clive is an odd one."

Chapter Seventeen

C live returns a few minutes later with a two cold cheese sandwiches packed with lettuce and tomatoes, and a bowl of
vegetable soup that we share. I didn't realize how hungry I was
until I found myself slurping up the entire bowl of soup and not
sharing any with him. He doesn't say anything though, and instead
pulls some chicken jerky from his pocket which he then shares
with his cats.

We work for a few more hours until I can't stop yawning and
Clive's arms are raw from the scratches inflicted on him by any the
more 'unwilling' of feline models. I have just enough fabric to make
Clive a simple, form fitting vest to match his furry performers
and then I find myself needing to call it a night. There's an actual
real bed waiting for me in my room and I can't wait to sleep on
something soft after my stay in the cold storage room.

"Just one more stitch here, so hold really still," I tell Clive as I
make one final adjustment to his vest.

"Everything looks really good and I mean that, Bluebell. It looks
really good. I can't believe how creative you are and how fast you
work, it's incredible."

"Shhh, hold still," I say through gritted teeth because I don't
want to ruin his kind words with a needle poke to his shoulder.

Finally, I lean back and admire my work. Clive does a twirl and probably because half his cats are trained performers, two of them leap to his shoulders and sit on either side while placing their tiny paws on top of his head.

The sight makes me laugh, but a yawn creeps in at the very end and Clive frowns.

"It's late, let me walk you back now," he says, gently removing the cats and gesturing toward the door.

"Thanks," I murmur, containing another yawn which makes him yawn and we both laugh.

The hallways are now quiet, but dimly lit by what appear to be candles along the walls. On closer inspection I see the flames are barely strips of colored plastic. Still, they breathe an authentic and older ambiance to this place that while still reminds me of my family's estate, it also speaks of history and humor and of Clive. I even detect notes of Flame within the walls as they remind me of what we always imagined large libraries to resemble.

I'm so lost in thought, that I barely register when we arrive on the Stage Girls floor, which is certainly not quiet. Clive grins as the lift doors open and I realize we had been walking in silence the entire way. Maybe he knew I had things to think about and memories to conjure.

"I think you can find your way from here?" he asks and I nod.

"Thank you," I tell him before he turns to leave. "I know it's just a scarf, but it means a lot to me, so thanks for your help."

Clive smiles and bows lowly once more and even though a few people pop their heads out of the dooryards and giggle at his silly gesture, we both ignore them. When he rises back up, he reaches for my hand and presses his lips to my knuckles as if I were like the beautiful woman found in a fairy tale garden from one of Flame's books.

"I'll see you tomorrow," he says just as the lift door closes and I'm left alone in the hall.

"Was that Kitty Cat Clive?" someone asks from my side and I turn to see the brown-haired girl who helped me wash dishes from earlier in the evening. I give her an exaggerated wink and she snickers in return.

"He's so weird!"

"You shouldn't talk about others like that." I shrug and move on down the hallway, not feeling up to the gossip.

When I finally make it to what I'm fairly certain is the room I'm now sharing with Minty and Butterscotch, I stop at the door because I notice it's closed. But it makes me notice that above the dooryard in a pretty swirling letter, someone has written my name just under the girls' names.

The pinch in my stomach relaxes just a little as I open the door quietly because for the first time in a while, I feel like I'm truly in a place where I belong.

There is a hum that halos around me when I open my eyes in the morning, and it is more than just the sound of Minty blow drying her golden curls at our one giant shared mirror. No, it is the air itself.

Even though a delicious anticipation grows in my stomach for the day to begin, I can't seem to pull myself out from under the warm bed sheets, eager to block out the world. I don't know if it was the steady movement of the train, the soft noises of the other girls reminding me that I am not alone, or the safety I've found within these walls, but my body just won't listen and I attempt to bury myself under the covers much like Butterscotch.

"Rise and shine!" screeches Minty when she notices my subtle movements. I hear a matching grumbling from the other cot and I know Butterscotch is struggling with waking as well. I didn't realize Minty was such a... morning person.

"Big day today," Minty chirps as she continues to work on her hair. "It's a performance day and I need to train you on what you'll be responsible for, as well as make sure you have time to get you over to the preshow performers."

"Why do I have to go there?" I ask, jumping down from my bed and stretching my back. Maybe I slept too well because my muscles are tightly wound as if I'm nervous, which I refuse to allow myself to be.

"Oh... well," Minty stalls, but Butterscotch has finally stood up and is pulling a brush through her own hair when she eyes Minty's twitching expression.

"What do you know that she doesn't?" she asks and I see Minty give a little shake before making eye contact with me.

"I've been awake for hours and got to the assignments before anyone else, looks like someone signed her up with the performers."

"What is that like?" I ask, covering a yawn with my hand. Memories from last night pop into my mind and I'm thinking about Clive's soft lips on my skin when Minty lets out an earsplitting laugh that causes Butterscotch to drop her brush.

"It means you'll do some light performing in front of an audience, probably in something before the main show begins. I heard
they sold over a thousand tickets for this one, so there will be a lot
of people passing through for the pre-show performances."

"Whew, that's a decent sized audience," breathes Butterscotch.
"But not as much as Main at least. What's she doing?"

"She's listed next to Clive, so probably something with the cats?"

"Wait, what? He didn't say anything about this last night! Do
you think he signed me up? And perform? I don't know how to
do anything!"

"Maybe it was Clive?" Butterscotch mumbles, rubbing her head
in thought. "I don't feel like he's the type to play a joke like that.
Kind of mean to make you do something like on what is basically
your first day. He would have had to approve it, though, so that
part is on him."

"Can't I just not do it? This has to be some mistake," I say,
rummaging around in a pile of donated clothes Minty brought for
me last night.

Luckily, I find a pair of soft grey pants that are long enough
to cover my legs and a snug black shirt without sleeves. I wish I
had some jewelry to complete the look. There's something about
a pulled together outfit that makes me feel powerful and from
my new friends' reactions, I think I need some of that sparkling
confidence.

Because this is the last thing I need. Performing in front of an
audience! What if I'm recognized and word gets back to Patrick
and Robbie? They could be out there right now just waiting to
grab me and drag me back...

"No, once you're signed up, you're signed up and there's no changing it or you'll risk getting fired," says Minty interrupting my thoughts. "I'll ask around and see what I can find out, but you'll need to do it. Look at it this way, though, some girls here have been trying and trying to get on stage and it's never happened because none of the performers approve of it. Just... try not to think about how many people are watching you."

"Well... great." I sigh, rubbing my tired eyes. They feel puffy and I wish I had some cooling lotion to put on them, but Minty and Butterscotch are dressed and ready to get to breakfast, so I find myself dragging my body after them.

The hum is still in the air and the energizing pull makes me temporarily forget the nervous stitch once again growing in my stomach. The dining floor is packed full of people and I find myself feeling extremely lucky for not having to clean up after this group. Food is being piled onto plates and shoved into my mouth at alarming rates, and I even catch the distinct whiff of bacon wafting by my nose.

"Swiney Acres select! Nothing but the best!" an excited Sally passes by and claps me on the shoulders. I give her a wan smile in return and continue after Minty as we make our way towards the quieter end of the long buffet.

Here, we scoop scrambled eggs studded with green onions onto our plates and grab small bowls filled with brightly colored fruits. Butterscotch even brings over a fresh pot of coffee and several cups. It's definitely not Flame's specially brewed cinnamon lattes, but once filled with a thick vanilla syrup that Minty swipes from the table next to us, it's almost as good.

Butterscotch notices my growing discomfort but true to the circus way, she doesn't pry. She instead tries to cheer me up by telling me how she completely failed at her RIS interview, but was taken on anyway because the circus was short on performers at the time. Soon into her story, Clive slides into the seat next to mine.

It's almost too natural as he jumps into the conversation and relates his own tales of watching the RIS interviews when he was younger. He, of course, never had to go through them because he's 'circus born and bred.'

"Are you ready for today?" he asks and I nearly choke on my coffee. I was starting to have a good time and nearly forgot about what I had in store for me later in the day.

"Did you have anything to do with this? I had no intention of getting up in front of that many people," I say and Clive cocks his head to the side and gives the girls a sideways look.

"She didn't sign up for it," Minty explains.

"We don't know who did," adds Butterscotch.

"Oh," Clive mutters, and if I didn't know any better, I'd say he looks disappointed. But whatever flashes across his face is gone in an instant because he suddenly smiles brightly. "Well, don't worry. We'll make the best of it!"

"You say that with so much confidence," I mumble into my coffee.

"That's because I'm a pretty confident guy," he tells me, nudging my ribs. "You just need some more coffee to be on my level and we'll do just fine."

"Is that even possible?" I ask and he shrugs.

"Eh, anything's possible when coffee is involved."

"You sound like my friend, Flame." I laugh.

"Then she must be a very smart girl, because I am also smart and talented and good looking if-I-do-say-so-myself." He huffs on his nails and buffs them on his shirt.

"Hmmm, maybe we should leave," teases Minty and Butterscotch nearly rolls out of her seat laughing. I'm about to help her back up when a shadow falls over our table and I look up to see someone I haven't met yet.

He looks serious and has a soft cover of closely cropped hair covering his head, as well as smudges of an unshaven face. He also looks as tired as I feel and his yawn is contagious as he flips a page over on a clipboard and looks down at Clive.

"Supper!" cries Clive, leaning back to look up at him. It puts his head against my chest and I don't find myself pulling away, but I do blush and attempt to not make eye contact with Minty who is snickering quietly.

"Clive," Supper says, in dry and annoyed voice.

"Supper," Clive repeats with a grin and Supper lets out the sigh of a man long suffering from who knows what. From the clipboard he's carrying and the way everyone seems to know him makes him look to be seemingly in charge around here. He glances down at me with a curious look in his eyes before looking back at Clive.

"I have to bump you to Main," he says, checking off something from a list on his clipboard. "Jonah has a sprained ankle."

Clive's smile wavers and I can see that Minty and Butterscotch's eyes have gone huge.

"You know I need more notice than that," he says, straightening up.

"You know how it is," Supper says, shrugging and checking something on his clipboard. "Second Tent for dress, but no cubby assignment."

Clive looks like he barely hears him as Supper rattles off a few additional names before leaving us to the remains of breakfast. I feel like the breakfast I just ate has formed into a stone and that it weighs on me as heavily as the ring in my pocket. I find myself nervously looking out the nearest window as if I could see the audience waiting for me just outside the safety of the land train.

"What exactly is 'Main'?" I ask the now very quiet table. "Is it what I think it might be?"

"Well," starts Clive, cracking his knuckles and giving me a long look. "Looks like we're performing in the main tent under the spotlight and that it's no small pre-show set up for us, darling. We're center stage today!"

Chapter Eighteen

I'm fairly certain my mouth drops open because Minty reaches over to push on my chin with her finger and gives me an encouraging smile.

I begin to wring my hands together. This is the worst possible thing! I shouldn't expose myself to that many people because someone is bound to recognize me and give word to my parents and the Lesters. That one lady, Sally, was able to do it, so there has to be some vendor or investor or worse, Robbie or Patrick themselves, waiting out there to grab me and haul me kicking and screaming all the way back to Pioneer Springs. What am I going to do?

"Don't worry, most people will be looking at the cats and not you," Clive finally says while standing up slowly.

"Um... thanks?" I manage, rubbing my hands over my arms to help ease the sickly feeling tingling all over my body. The pit in my stomach grows once more until I'm full of nothing but breakfast and the dark, scary thoughts of marriage into the Lester family, and I bend into myself.

"Looks like someone has a bit of stage fright," Minty says unhelpfully and looks towards Clive. "You better make sure to take good care of her."

"I promise that I shall," he tells her and gently takes my elbow, steering me to my feet and then to stand beside him. "But we'll need to get going if that's going to happen."

I follow his movements numbly and barely register when Minty and Butterscotch tell me to break a leg out there, and Sally passes by with the very last of the bacon. Even the sweet and smokey smell of it can't break me from my comatose state, but once we're in the lift headed to who knows where, I'm able to focus on the one thing in front of me in this moment. Clive.

"I'm scared," I whisper and he looks at me after the doors hiss shut.

"Why? It'll be okay. You'll just have to stand here and hold still. I mean, sometimes the cats get a little feisty and might scratch you just a little, but they mostly don't leave permanent scars." He seems to realize his comment and clears his throat, his eyes darting away from the red skin around my neck.

True to Sally's word, the injury inflicted upon me by Robbie has left a long thin scar running along my neck like a tight fitting necklace. The healing salve was like magic and I don't even feel it anymore, but I know it's there because it's the first thing I look at whenever I come across a mirror.

"It's not the performing part, well maybe a little of that. There's just something you should know..." I start and Clive raises an eyebrow as he waits for me to continue, but the lift doors open before us and we're forced out into the bright sun of a new day.

The air and light and scents and sound nearly make me stumble back, but Clive's hard chest gets in the way and he holds me upright. I realize I've been so used to the dry, desolate air of Pioneer

Springs that I never gave much thought to what other cities would be like and I'm shocked by what I see before me.

"This is Searless?" I gasp and Clive nods, throwing both arms out in a grand gesture before him.

"This is nothing!" he confirms and laughs. "Well, yes, it is Searless, but if you're this shocked by a kind of place like this, just wait till we get closer to the coastlines."

Pioneer Springs is an old city, and while there is a certain kind of sad beauty coming from the Dusting, it always felt like what it was: just a stopover place. Somewhere you come by, do some shopping, maybe visit someone you know or take in the sights of a place that close to the messy world beyond. But this place. This is a place where people live.

Even from where we stand, which is next to the giant land train, I notice we're located on a small hill and that the city proper sprawls out before us like the most elegant and colorful quilt ever imaginable. It must be fantastic in the nighttime when all the solar powered street lamps come alive. I can just imagine them as diamonds of color sparkling against the blackened sky, as if the world itself was wearing earrings made from a thousand crystals.

I turn to Clive and find him staring at me in wonder, but he looks away quickly and points down a dusty pathway. I try to wipe away the look of awe I know is planted on my face because I have much bigger things to worry about right now.

"I brought the cats down already. It's always better to bring them out before everyone else gets up and about. We'll meet up with them, get dressed and then it'll be showtime before you know it."

The flushed excitement drains from my face and leaves nothing but a blank white canvas. Clive notices and puts a reassuring hand on the small of my back as he pushes me forward.

"Come on, pig heiress, you jumped onto a moving train after something nearly tried to strangle you, I think you can do this."

"It's not that," I breathe. "I'm scared they'll find me."

Clive cocks his head to the side as he looks at me, then takes my hand and pulls me down the path with him.

"Well, all the better we get inside Second Tent," he says lightly and I can't tell if he's taking me seriously or poking fun.

It's a short walk, or maybe it's quick because we're walking pretty fast, but we arrive soon at a big purple striped tent. I almost don't enter, the last tent I walked into wasn't the best experience, but Clive goes first and drags me with him. But inside this tent there are no chicken ladies squabbling over what I'm wearing and who I'm marrying, but something completely different.

We enter through a stiff door made from the head curtain fabric and it falls behind us, covering the exit completely. The only light is that glowing beyond the purple fabric and gives everything a pink filter. A short hallway stretches before us and has four separate doors, two off either side, until it stops at the other end with a second door leading outside.

Clive points to one of the doors that someone has attached a small sign of a cat jumping through a hoop.

"That's us," he says softly and pushes me towards it. I take a big gulp of air and try to steady my breathing because the reality of performing has settled my chest like, well, a heavy cat sitting on my chest.

I step inside and find a room roughly the size of Clive's two bedrooms. One side is set up with a series of metal cages, each with a cat inside and opposite them is an expansive table set up with various makeups and a large mirror set behind it. A rack of clothing completes the space and I notice a box beneath containing the new pieces I contrasted with Clive last night.

"Ready to get ready?" Clive sings behind me and I turn to him and try to smile, but instead, I break down in tears.

"That is not the kind of reaction I was hoping for," Clive says not unkindly, guiding me to the makeup table. He then hoists me up by my waist, which I don't have any strength to struggle out of, and sets me on the table so that we're eye to eye.

"Do you want to talk about it?" he asks and I fidget with the hem of my sleeve instead of answering.

"I'm scared."

"Sometimes the cats are scared so I don't make them perform. Do you need to sit out?" he asks and I shake my head.

"No, I don't want to make any trouble for you. You've been so kind. It's just... I'm afraid someone will recognize me."

"Embarrassed to be performing with Kitty Cat Clive?" he asks lightly as if he was joking, but I can tell from the way his brows furrow that the thought must bother him.

"No, someone from my family or the family of the man I was supposed to marry, the guy who did this," I say, pointing at my neck.

Clive frowns as I shrug my shoulders and wipe my face with my sleeve until he hands me a handkerchief to dry my tears.

"My parents and older brother wanted me to marry this guy named Robbie Lester and he...well, it wouldn't have been a smooth marriage. He wanted me for my ties to the pig factory and my family wanted him for his ties to the chicken industry. No one really seemed to care what I wanted, so I ran away before they could make me go through with it."

"At least you got out before the wedding."

"Just barely, if I had stuck around ten extra minutes, I wouldn't have been so lucky."

Clive blows out a low and long whistle and runs a hand through his hair.

"A runaway bride, huh? You know, you should write all this down and bring it to the tumblers. It sounds like it would make a great story to tell on the trapeze."

"My life isn't some story," I tell him, but truthfully, my chest feels a little lighter after confiding in him and I give him a weak smile.

"Everyone's life is a story," he says with one of his heart melting smiles in return. "Some are just more beautiful and tragic than others and make for good storytelling."

"But what I am going to do about today's show? I can't get fired yet, I don't have any money or where to go. I don't know what to do!"

"You'll hide in plain sight, that's the best possible thing in this sort of impossible situation," Clive tells me and gestures for me to come off the table and sit in a chair that's been propped up against the tent wall.

"Huh?" I gasp, feeling as stupid as I'm sure the expression on my face appears, but I follow his instructions and sit down in the chair.

"No one will recognize you in costume," he says in his sing-song voice. "Well, the cats will, but that's because they have such a keen sense of smell. So don't worry your pretty little head about it, Clive will take care of it."

"Hmm, the last guy I trusted let me down big time," I say softly, unable to keep the edge of sadness from creeping into my voice. Clive notices and after grabbing two containers of white and black face paint from the table, he comes over and lifts my chin up to face him.

"Who let you down?" he asks.

"His name was Milo. He was my bodyguard and friend and I thought he might have been more. But I was wrong and he wouldn't come with me when I left," I whisper.

Clive dips his fingers into the white paint and swirls it around before saying, "He didn't stop you though. I think being able to let someone go and be on their own without you is one of the highest forms of trust."

I squeeze my eyes shut to keep from crying, but find myself nodding along with his words. When I open them again, it is to Clive's face directly in front of mine. I'm too stunned to breathe as I am lost in the deep blue of his eyes. We stay like that for a few moments, our breaths eventually synchronizing. I think even our hearts are beating that same fast and frantic rhythm of the kind of attraction you don't want to put into words. Because once you put it out there in the open, there is no turning back.

"I need you to hold still," he finally says. "I'm going to put a lot of face paint on you and tie back your hair before you get dressed."

"Okay," is the only word I can get out because he's suddenly straddling my lap. He's still standing, so there is a good distance between us, but with one long leg on either side of my thigh, I feel trapped by his massive chest. He then leans in with both hands and starts swiping white paint slowly up my neck with both hands, his palms lightly pressing into the thin skin below my jawline and working their way up along my cheeks. He dips his fingers in more paint and soon he's painted my entire face a smooth white color that he then accents with patches of black.

Afterward, he wipes off his hands quickly and swings the chair around so he's standing behind me and I'm facing the curtain wall. He slathers a thick cream into my hair that smells like roses before he begins brushing the curls into a fine smoothness. I find myself leaning into his hands and closing my eyes at the tingling sensation in both my scalp and core.

"Did I tell you why I'm not a tumbler like the rest of my family?" he asks, breaking the silence and slapping me back to my senses.

"I think you said you didn't like it? Or something like that."

"Correct, but the real reason is that I never felt a calling. To do that kind of crazy stuff in the air, something has to ask you, actually beg you, to fly through it. The very stars need to call your name and make you join them in the sky." He pauses while smoothing my hair out in a long tail and his fingers tickle the back of my neck while he secures it with a shiny red ribbon. "What I'm getting at is that you need to listen to that voice inside you, it may just be whispering right now but eventually it will start yelling if you don't pay attention to it. And that voice is what guides you to your dreams, or at least to your next adventure."

"I think your voice got it wrong for you, it sounds like you should be a poet instead of a circus clown," I tease as he spins me and the chair around from the tent's wall. We only have eyes for each other right now and he gives me a bold wink before moving away.

"Aren't clowns and poets one and the same? We both perform our dreams for others," he says, grabbing an outfit from the rack of clothing and handing it to me. "But enough talk about voices and stars, people think I'm crazy enough as it is. We need to get dressed, which means I need you to put this on and then help me dress the cats."

"What exactly am I doing out there?" I ask, dread and fear once again pooling in my stomach and I see Clive give me a wicked grin.

"Take a look in the mirror and get dressed, it's pretty obvious."

I raise an eyebrow at him, but walk over to the mirror to look at his work. Then I look at the outfit he handed me, then back at my face and then back at the outfit and one more time at my face. The black and white face paint, my smooth hair tied tight with a red bow and a black and white spotted jumpsuit, oh pig farts... I'm going to be dressed as a...

If I didn't think it would startle both the cats and every single person within a hundred-yard radius, I would scream at him, but I instead let out a strained growl that vibrates up my spine as I hiss, "You're dressing me up as a cow?"

Chapter Nineteen

S ome of the things Clive says to me on our way out of the tent:

"It'll be perfect, no one will recognize you."

"You pull off black and white spots quite well."

"If anyone asks for a picture, charge them two dollars."

"You sure make a pretty heifer."

My responses to him are not nearly as nice, still, he makes a good point and I doubt Robbie, Patrick, my parents, or literally anyone from Pioneer Springs would recognize their Pig Heiress dressed as a cow. It'd probably be considered a clash of interests or something.

We're pushing two large containers in front of us, full of cats by the way, and happen to pass by a group of Stage Girls. Luckily, Rose is not among them, but I do recognize a few of her friends and I can tell by the snickering that they can't wait to relay the news to her. They even 'moo' at me as we walk by.

"Ignore them, you are breathtaking," Clive says.

"Moo," I answer.

It's a short walk to a small side entrance to the main tent and Clive explains it's done on purpose for the cats, but whenever I peak under the heavy flaps protecting their cages, none of them look fazed by what's waiting for us on the other side of the big striped tent in front of us.

"They've trained for this," Clive tells me, sticking a finger in through the flaps and cooing at the cats inside.

"So, what do I do in there?" I ask.

"Act like a cow? I'm not sure, I didn't really think this part through."

"Wait, you're just going to fake your way through a performance on the main stage?" I poke my head inside the flap to look at what I'm up against and come back out gasping for air. "In front of the entire city of Searless?"

"It'll work out, it always does. The trick with animal performers is that you kind of have to do what they want to do. Sure, I give them vague instructions, but they're the real stars of the show."

I can hear music swelling before us and I know we don't have a whole lot of time and I begin to bounce on my heels and flex my hands. My palms are slick with sweat as I look at Clive. He must see the panic in my eyes because he puts a reassuring hand on my shoulder.

"Just breathe and if I kiss you in there, please don't jump over the moon," he says with his trademark, heart melting smile.

"Wait... what?" I start, but don't have time because the tent flaps suddenly spring open before us. Clive urges me forward with my cage of cats and have no choice but to hurry after him.

Our slot is scheduled after a fifteen-minute interlude between the bigger acts and the audience, freshly poured back into their seats, watches us with eager anticipation. The smell of salted popcorn is heavy in the electrified air and I gaze around in wonder at rows of seating that seem to stretch on forever. Even if I knew someone within this massive crowd, there would be no way for me to pick them out. From here, everyone is one giant blur.

Someone has set up a series of small tree stumps, each a different color, and poles topped with flat squares of wood in various sizes dot the ring. Several hoops are suspended on tall poles between the taller of the platforms and a pile of extra ones lays off to the side.

Clive suddenly bumps into me from behind and proceeds to pretend to have a very hard time pushing me from my spot, much to the delight of the audience who begins laughing right away. I roll my eyes at him. Not like anyone out there could see such a gesture, and stamp my feet several times in annoyance. He scratches his head in thought and pushes the cage forward without my help. As he passes, I can tell the cats are eagerly pacing inside.

He maneuvers the second cage next to the first and gestures for me to come forward, but when I try to move, I find my legs are shaking too much and I stumble forward awkwardly. The crowd takes it as part of the act and laughs as Clive plods over to me, crosses his arms and pretends to look me over as if there was something defective about the creature standing in front of him.

And that's when I remember that I'm a cow. I pretended to amble away from him and stood with my back turned, admiring a patch of dirt on the ground that may or may not had grass at some point in time. I can feel him coming up behind me and spring up at the last second as if something else caught my attention and he stumbles dramatically, waving his hands in the air as if to catch himself on an imaginary chair.

"Moo!" I turn around and yell, then just in case anyone can't hear me, I stick my tongue out and sit down on one of the nearby stumps. It causes the audience to break into laughter and I sit there soaking it in. Maybe this won't be so bad after all. But Clive gives me a wicked grin when he notices that I'm sitting on one of the colored stumps and in one swift movement, he opens the first cage and five cats come leaping out, Michelle and Bruno included.

One by one, each cat leaps onto a designated colored stump until the last, mighty and hefty Bruno spies that his stump is occupied by none other than the lady who made him wear his silly little golden costume. I don't know if cats are vindictive, but he looks at me and I look at him while the audience watches both of us with bated breath. Clive cackles along the sidelines.

"Purrrrpt!" Bruno lets out a meow that the audience possibly could hear and does a flying leap into my arms, trusting me to both catch and hang onto his considerable weight.

"Oooff," I wheeze as he lands on my shoulders while the audience claps. He basks in their attention and I wonder how long I'm going to have to support him as he swishes his tail in my face.

I can't see what else is happening thanks to the fluffy tail, but the audience is loving it and eventually I hear Clive come closer to us and feel Bruno leap off my shoulders to a small platform he holds up above his head. The leaping cat's force causes me to lose my balance on the stump and I fall over on my backside, which the audience roars in laughter and Clive sneaks me an apologetic look.

He has Bruno jump from the platform through one of the raised hoops a few times, until I guess Bruno has had enough attention for one day and returns to the inside of his cage, leaving only pretty Michelle sitting on another platform off to the side. She cleans her face with her slender paws, but keeps peering at Clive with intense, yellow eyes.

Clive gives a low and overly dramatic bow to the audience, who laugh and clap for him and his cats, and then he gestures for me to get up and join him. When I do, the audience claps even louder and it's the most amazing, indescribable feeling. Never in my life have I done something like this and the appreciation and thrill of people applauding me brings tears to my eyes.

Clive bows lowly once more and drapes his hands over my shoulders to force me into the bow as well. When we rise back up, he flips his arms around and dips me low, bending his face towards mine like in the covers of so many of Flame's romance novels. He really is going to kiss me in front of all these people!

Caught up in the moment, I close my eyes but then I feel him snap his fingers behind my back and in a flash, Michelle leaps onto my chest and sits with her butt on my face. It causes Clive's lips to land squarely on the side of her cheek.

And the audience loses it, laughing and cheering so loud that as soon as Clive spins us back up and Michelle leaps off to return to the cage, I have to cover my ears from the noise. Clive winks at me and gestures grandly towards the cages and then, as the lights dim around us and the crowd prepares to welcome another act, I give one more quick bow and hurry to help him push the cages back outside the tent.

Once the tent flaps close, the late afternoon descends upon us and the sunny sky makes me feel dizzy and tired. I tilt my head back and close my eyes, letting the light shine directly onto my face, and even though the sunbeams have to travel through thick layers of cow paint, I feel them enter my skin to seep into my blood and warm me from within.

When I open my eyes, it's to Clive staring at me but he blushes and turns away quickly once he sees me notice him. The sunlight catches on his new gold vest and he glows like some sort of mythical inhuman creature, too perfect for this world, and I feel the stirrings of attraction pull at my heart. But when he looks back up and catches me staring, it's my turn to blush and turn away. There might be something there, but I'm too much of a chicken to find out.

"You did really good out there," he says as we continue pushing the cat cages towards the nearby land train.

"I guess, for a cow."

"No, I really mean it. It takes a certain ability to act with animals, you have to be very good at impromptu situations and making things up as you go along, all while making sure everyone watching things you know exactly what you're doing."

"Sounds like life," I say and Clive laughs in return.

"You're very right in that, but enough of this cute banter, we need to get these guys inside and fed before they tear this cage apart."

I follow Clive along the pathway, pushing the now vibrating cage of cats before me. He has them trained well and I'm pretty sure that just like the pigs at Swiney Acres, they know when it's time to eat and have absolutely no shame in screaming for their supper.

He takes us to one of the larger lifts towards the back and opens up a small concealed panel to call the lift to us, and we stand in companionable silence while we wait.

A breeze kicks up in the air and draws my attention away from the swaying cages and the small wisps of Clive's sandy hair along his neck, and I find myself looking out past the land train. The purple and white striped tent takes up much of the land we're parked on and while not as big as the land train, it doesn't leave a whole lot of room for much else, but there is a smaller set of tents off to the side and I think I remember Clive telling me those are the cubbies, smaller areas where some performers hang out for tips after the performances.

But beyond those I can see the remains of concession stands and a few smaller stages and workers among them are what I think might be the Stage Girls and some performers.

Clive notices my gaze and leans in to whisper, "They begin taking everything down during the last of the major acts in the center ring. Then after the show, people have no choice but to go home or hang around and visit the cubbies."

I nod along as he points out a smaller stage almost completely taken apart by now and tells me that he normally performs there because the big top isn't the most ideal place for small cat performers, but something else about it has caught my attention.

A group of girls who look a little familiar are carrying various wooden sections between themselves and I recognize the brown-haired girl who helped me wash dishes, she's chatting with a tall man and gesturing widely with her arms. A few other girls have also put down their various stage pieces and have come over too. The man has his back turned to me, but there is something about the way he is dressed that doesn't quite match with what I've seen around here.

No, this is an expensive suit, much grander than anything even Snuzzle would own, and his hair is perfectly styled over his square shoulders. The brown-haired girl is pointing at the land train now and explaining something and as she does, the man turns in our direction and I spin around before he can make any sort of eye contact with me.

A cold sweat beads on my forehead and it isn't from the warm and sunny air, but it's my body's reaction to trying to unfreeze the cold pit that is forming in my stomach because I think I know the man.

"Are you okay?" Clive asks. "The lift will be here any second and we'll get inside, I know it's pretty hot out there."

"It's not that," I hiss. "Don't look, but over there by the stages, there's a man talking to the girls. Is he watching us?"

"I wouldn't know because you told me not to look, but I can tell you that no one is coming towards us right now and we're alone," he says in his sing-song voice. He stretches his arms up high above his head and leans casually against the side of the train with his back pressed against the hard steel. "There, now I'm watching your back. But it looks like whoever that was talking to them is gone. I don't see anyone I don't know."

There's a small ding as the lift arrives and I hurry to push the cats inside and wave Clive in after me. He pushes his group of cages in and stands by my side as we watch the lift doors close.

"Bluebell, what's wrong?" he asks, reaching out and taking my hand. He holds it to his chest and looks into my eyes. I don't know how to react, but his warm hands and the soft beating of his heart help ease the tension in my heart.

"I think that was my brother," I whisper so softly that maybe only the cats can hear me, but because Clive is probably part cat, he nods in understanding and gives my hands a squeeze.

"We'll keep you safe, the circus looks after their own."

Chapter Twenty

I move my hands away from his and to the cage because I need to steady myself. My chest squeezes painfully as my fists grip the cage bars until my knuckles turn white. I don't say a word as the lift, one of the slower and larger ones, takes us to Clive's level and all the while, I stare at the floor.

My mind tumbles into awful scenarios that all end poorly for me. Patrick dragging me out by my hair and throwing me into the back of a solar car, speeding away through the highways and back to my old life. Patrick coming to tell me there has been a horrible accident and the entire town of Pioneer Springs has been swallowed by the Dusting. Patrick telling me that Robbie is here for my hand in marriage and he will not leave until I see it through.

Clive keeps quiet, seemingly knowing that I'm processing something heavy on my mind, but I catch him looking at me when I finally raise my head and his face is a mixture of concern and curiosity. He moves around his cage so that he's standing in front of me.

"Breathe with me," he says softly, peeling my hands away from the bars and placing them at my sides. "I find it helps when I have too much going on all at once and all over the place."

"I'm just nervous, if that really was Patrick down there and I think it was, why is he here? Is he here alone? Is Robbie here? Or Milo? I don't want to go back there..."

"Focus on breathing with me," Clive says again. He holds a hand up between us and makes a fist. "When I spread my fingers, I want you to breathe in and when I close my fist, breathe out and hold your breath. Only release when my hand opens again and you can breathe in again. Got it?"

I give him a small nod and watch his hand. And even though there is a heavy curtain between us, it feels like the cats are watching too and waiting for Clive to begin.

Then amid the gently swaying and quiet lift, Clive slowly opens his fist and I follow his instructions by breathing in deeply and only out again as his hand slowly closes itself once more. He repeats the process a few times, following along with his own breath, and I find I'm concentrating so hard on the process that most of my dark thoughts slink away back into the darkness from where they came.

But life isn't that simple and while I feel better when Clive stops, I still feel a pressuring pull of unease deep within my body.

"Let's get the cats put away and fed, then we'll toil away at making a plan," he says before raising a hand to brush away a strand of my hair. He stops midway, almost as if he isn't sure if I'll allow the touch, but I lean into it instead and let him push it behind my ear. I'm focusing on the way his fingers feel as they trail along my skin and leave a delicious and tingling sensation as they go, but when he pulls them back and I notice they're smudged in white and black paint, another sensation starts to bubble inside. I erupt in a deep belly laugh that makes me double over when I realize I'm still painted and dressed like a cow.

So very romantic, Flame would joke if she was here.

"I need a shower," I tell Clive, wiping a tear away but finding my own hand covered in face paint which makes me laugh again. He is laughing with me and we don't even notice the lift arrives on his floor and reveals someone standing directly in the doorway.

"What is so ridiculously funny?" Rose asks, stepping aside so Clive and I can push the rolling cages forward and into the posh hallway of the Clown floor. Once again, the doors to the rooms are all tight, but there are still the sounds of several violins playing down the hallway. The cats must hear it and know they are almost home and almost about to be fed, because they've suddenly begun to move around inside their cages and were making demanding cat noises at us.

"Nothing," I giggle, wiping the paint off on Clive's cow suit and hoping I can get it washed later. "What are you doing here? This isn't your floor."

"I was looking for you," says Rose, crossing her arms over her chest. "Seems like I was wrong about it, maybe you can hold your own around here."

"I didn't realize anyone was doubting that I could," I tell her, moving to stand between her and the cat cages. Clive is at my back and while I know I must look utterly - udderly - silly dressed as a cow in front of her, I find a sense of pride and determination blossoming in my chest as I stand up to her.

But Rose waves me off and gives me a rare smile that almost looks genuine. "It was actually, and I hate to admit this, a really good act. I was off to the sides with concessions and we could all see how much the audience loved it. I didn't think you had it in you, pig heiress. I'm impressed."

"Um, thank you?"

"But anyway, you won our bet and I owe you your friend's scarf. Come with me to my room and I'll get it for you."

"I have to help Clive get the cats back," I say and Rose makes a face.

"No, you don't. He's been doing this on his own for years, haven't you, Clive?" she says.

Clive shifts on his feet a few times as he looks at her, then to me and then to the cats. "Yeah, I'll be fine."

"Good! Come on then, I need to get out of here soon. They're letting us have a night out on town before we leave in the morning and I want to get an early start!"

"Sure," I stammer as she pulls me inside a smaller lift next to the one, we arrived in and just as the lift doors begin to close, I yell back at Clive that I'll catch up with him later, but the doors are quick and I don't get a chance to hear his response.

This lift is faster than the last, but it still takes us a few minutes before it gets to the Stage Girl's floor and I realize this is the first time I've been alone with Rose since she helped sneak me onto the train.

I still don't know what to make of her, but I think it a good sign if she's willing to hold up her end of the bargain. Perhaps we're not destined to be friends in this lifetime, but I think I can at least be a good person to her if she's willing to do the same for me. Then, as if she can read my mind, she hands over a package of moist face towelettes so that I can wipe the majority of cow makeup off my face. I take them from her gratefully and use the shiny metal lift walls as a mirror.

"That's to thank you for that gum," she says and I chuckle.

After most of the 'cow' is gone from my features and about a minute of total silence, I decide to try and use this time to my advantage and see if she knows anything about the person downstairs asking questions. Maybe she got his name.

"Hey, I saw someone downstairs asking some of the girls questions, do you know what he wanted?" I ask her.

"There was a man downstairs?" Rose asks in a startled voice that sounds mildly authentic. "No, I don't think anyone said anything and I certainly didn't see him. Why?"

"Oh, no reason, really. I just thought he looked familiar and wanted to see if it was someone I knew."

"Do you meet a lot of people being a pig heiress?" Rose laughs.

"Actually, the very opposite," I say back to her, but any future conversation between us is cut off as soon as the lift opens unexpectedly onto a silent floor. Curious, I step out on the floor and gasp in astonishment.

I barely register the soft thud of the lift door closing behind me as we both look down the long hallway. What is usually a busy, cluttered and noisy area is eerily quiet and vacant of all life, even the doors are shut tight. Rose reaches over and grips my upper arm tightly, moving me to the side of the lift and near a small, sectioned off area. Without a word, she begins tapping on something on the wall and I lean in close.

"What's going on?" I whisper, sensing the urgency in her posture and the frantic way she taps at the small side panel she's pulled down from the wall.

"I don't know, but something isn't right," she says quietly. "Watch my back, I can't remember the password to this thing and it keeps locking me out."

"What is that?"

"It's another way out of here besides the lift, once it stops on a sealed floor like this, the lift won't budge again, at least not from this side. Security can still get in," Rose mumbles, still taping in codes.

"Why would it be sealed?" I'm unable to keep my voice from shaking and Rose turns to me with a hard expression on her face.

"It means someone set off an alarm. Maybe your roommates haven't shown you yet, but there's a switch you can turn on if there's trouble. It'll call a security detail, but this place is big and you have to hide out until they come. Sometimes someone bends the rules and brings a boy or girl up here and things get out of hand and they have to flip the switch." The panel in front of her beeps a warning and she lets out a string of hard to hear curses. I look away to give her a moment and wonder if Minty and Butterscotch are okay. One of the hallway doors opens suddenly and a man steps out.

"There you are," a cold and familiar voice slides down the hallway like a snake in the bone fields and I look across and into the eyes of none other than Robbie Lester. He's wearing the nice suit I saw on the man down below and there's now no doubt in my mind that it was him I saw talking to the Stage Girls and not Patrick.

My palms begin to sweat and as I'm wiping them on the cow suit, I tug on Rose's sleeve to alert her. She turns and looks over at him.

"I know you..." she says, straightening up and peering intently at Robbie, who hasn't come over to us yet and seems to rather be enjoying himself over my discomfort. "You're the guy who left me high and dry in Pioneer Springs."

Robbie gives Rose a long look as if he's deciding if he wants to remember her or not, but a slow smile spreads across his ugly face.

"You're the circus girl!" he cries out, his voice dripping with the kind of stuck-up malice only he can bring to a conversation. "Dodged a bullet on that one. Glad to see you made it home safely though."

"Do you know him?" I turn and ask Rose and her cheeks turn scarlet.

"We were hanging out the night before the circus left Pioneer Springs, but once he found out who I was, he turned his nose up at me and left after making some excuse about attending a wedding."

"That was our wedding!" I growl, turning towards Robbie who couldn't look any happier. I feel Rose falter at my side and grip my arm once more.

"What are you talking about?" she asks.

"My family was making me marry this pile of chicken scat, but I got away from they could hog tie me and drag me to the altar. He was with you the night before the wedding?"

Rose's mouth falls open as the realization falls upon her, but a fury takes over her eyes that could terrify a normal person, but I recognize it as the same kind of determination and desperation I had when escaping my forced engagement. She turns quickly to the panel and in a flash, she taps in a successful code and a side panel in the wall slides open, exposing a way out for us. She turns to Robbie.

"You're disgusting," she snarls. He hasn't moved towards us, but I can tell from the bunching of his shoulders that he's about to.

"How did you even get up here?" I ask, trying to stall as Rose works open a thin screen just beyond the open panel door.

"Some girl let me in," he says, vaguely gesturing behind him at the row of closed doors. "Didn't take much convincing to get her to show me around."

"Where is she now?"

"Behind one of these doors," he says with a deep scowl. "Pushed me out when I started demanding she take me to you. Then one by one all the doors slammed shut and locked, then out popped you two, so I guess it all worked out in my favor."

"Well, it's been just a pleasure seeing you again, Robbie, but it's a bad time for us and we're going to have to catch up later," Rose says, grabbing my shoulders and pushing me through the opening in the wall. She follows quickly behind, but isn't quick enough to escape Robbie's lunging form as he grabs at her legs.

She fumbles forward and flails her feet, trying to shake him, but he doesn't let go until I reach my own foot back through and give his knuckles a swift and heavy blow. I feel the satisfying crunch of bone as his hand goes limp and Rose's leg is free. She kicks the door shut in his face, then struggles to her feet and starts dragging me down the thin passageway.

"Come on, we need to get out of here fast because that panel behind us doesn't lock!"

Chapter Twenty-One

We charge through the winding passage and I wonder how Rose seems to know her way around, but don't have any time to ask her. I assume, though, it's from sneaking on and off the train so many times.

There are no stairs to climb up or down as we twist our way through the passage, so I know we're on the same high level, but I still have no idea where we could be or what is on the other side of these walls.

Rose, however, seems to know. And even though I trip and stumble behind her, I rush after her closely, even bumping into her back a few times. We begin to hear the huffing and puffing of someone else close on our heels, and try to pick up speed. My breathing feels stuck in my chest and I find it hard to catch my breath as we run. We're both smaller than Robbie and it's easier for us to dodge the beams and wires we come across, but he's strong and fast and I know there's no way we could outrun him.

Finally, we come to another wall, but this one has a small lever that Rose pulls quickly and she drags me through the opening. The room we fall into takes my breath away because it is windy and cold and empty save for building materials, some furniture, and lots of wiring.

Looking around, I see the reason for the cool and breezy air is that it's missing several large windows along the side. It makes my palms sweat to think about the sheer drop that could await someone if they got too close and I don't dare venture too close, even if I know the view is stunning. A pretty and expansive horizon is not worth my life.

"I don't know where to go from here," Rose tells me, her eyes wide and fearful as she paces the room.

"Where are we?" I ask and she begins wringing her hands when she looks over to answer. It's such a stark contrast to what I've seen from her since we first met, this Rose has lost all her arrogance and looks like a scared child.

"It's an older section of the train that they've been working on. It's taking forever, but eventually there will be more rooms for the Stage Girls so not everyone has two or three roommates," she answers, her voice trailing off as she continues to pace and becomes lost in thought.

I take a deep breath and close my eyes to concentrate. I flex my fingers and close them into fists as I try to slow my racing heart and clear my mind to focus on what we can do. The first breath tells me we need help and the second is that we need to buy some time.

If this place will be a copy of the Stage Girl rooms, what do I know about them that could be useful? Then I try to remember what Rose said about the lockdown before we ran here and I think I know what to do. When I open my eyes, I can also hear footsteps coming from the direction we came and know Robbie will be here soon. I get close to Rose and force her to pay close attention to my words by gripping her shoulders tightly.

"Okay, first things first, we need to block that door to buy us some time," I tell her and she nods, snapping back into the present and then helping me look for something to prop against the door we came through. We find a few chairs that we stack up, but we know they won't hold for very long. A lift off to the side also proves useless when we try to summon it. It only makes a low beeping noise in our faces and remains motionless.

"You said they're converting this area to more rooms, right?"

Rose nods.

"Mirror copies of the other rooms?"

She nods again.

"And you said all the rooms have an emergency switch to call for help, do you think they got that far already? There's a lot of wiring going on in here so maybe one of the switches works."

Rose looks around with a wild look in her eyes and we frantically search the room around until she freezes and points out a cluster of wires very near one of the gaping holes to our side.

"Of course it would be there," I mutter and I see her visually swallow as we look at the large, open window.

I can tell her legs are shaking worse than mine because she drops to the ground and clutches her knees to her chest and it falls on me to be the brave one. Robbie is banging loudly on the panel door now and it echoes through the empty room, making our plight feel even more dangerous.

I take one deep and centering breath to ground my thoughts because I don't have time to do a whole breathing exercise. Then, leaving Rose huddled on the ground by the unmoving lift doors, I walk to the window's ledge. The closer I get, the louder the air seems to rush at me. Cold air wipes my face and makes me wonder how high we are, it must be at least ten stories high.

Pioneer Springs is a fairly flat town and the biggest thing they have to their name is the giant land train station, but this beast is even taller than even that. Surely a plunge out these open windows would mean certain death, even if we're not at the very top. Still, I have to admit the view is breathtaking as I can see the late afternoon sun just beginning to edge the western horizon. The blues, pinks and purples would make a beautiful fabric for a dress.

I edge over to the bundle of wires and see there are two red switches, both connected to a couple of wire bundles that have their tail ends sticking through holes cut into the floor. I swallow hard and flip one of them, hoping that I'll hear some sort of sound to let me know it went live, but it's completely silent. A cold sweat drips down my back as I reach for the second, hoping this one is connected.

Robbie's banging on the door increases and is followed by the screeching sound of the chairs as they fall against the hard floor. He bursts through the panel door at last and stops to wipe dust and debris from his nicely pressed suit and as he does, I flip the second switch quickly, but can't hear any reaction over the sounds of Robbie bursting into the room.

Even though it goes against my desperate need for survival, I hold my ground and do not move towards him even if that means I'm still by the open window. I do turn around, though, so that I can face him and he won't be able to run up behind me and push me out. Out of the corner of my eye, I see Rose has stood up as well and is leaning against the wall beside the lift, frozen in place.

She seemed like such a hard person when I first met her, but seeing her facing a threat firsthand tells me there is some humanity in here. After all, she could have left me behind and escaped by herself through the passageway, she didn't have to take me. That's the circus way, I guess, you take care of your own.

"You!" Robbie hisses, spit flying from his mouth as he points a finger at me. Up close, I can see now that the suit, while still nicely pressed is dirty and caked with mud around his feet. His hair is an absolute mess and it looks like he hasn't slept since I last saw him, which would have only been a few days ago. Robbie looks dreadfully awful!

"What happened to you?" I ask. I don't know if I need to stall for time because there's no way to tell if the switch I flipped triggered any alarms. I feel like I need to keep him talking. If anything, maybe Rose will snap out of her trance and help somehow.

"What happened to me?" he repeats in a high-pitched voice that I assume is a mocking version of my own. "You happened to me. If you hadn't run away, none of this would have happened."

"Okay, no, I am in no way responsible for anything happening to you. Go home, Robbie, you'd never make it here in the circus."

"Home?" he scoffs. "I don't have a home to go back to. Your little idiot of a bodyguard, Milo, secured the station's surveillance footage before I could scrub it, and showed it to my parents. It was all over after that! He threatened to turn it in, to have me of all people arrested. I should have had that fool of a man taken care of long ago, but I let him run around town because it meant I didn't have to worry about someone taking you. But that was my mistake because you managed to kidnap yourself anyway!"

"The station's surveillance footage? You mean the video of you trying to kill me?" I spit back at him. At the same time I hear Rose gasp at my commission, something shifts behind me and I glance back to see one of the wires has shifted from the wind and is now dangling out the open window.

"You're just lucky I had some connections and funds secured in case of any... trouble like this," says Robbie. "I used it to catch up to you so quickly and easily. Seems like you've made a pretty little name for yourself among these freaks."

"None of us are freaks!" Rose finally says, she hasn't moved from the wall, but she's crossed her arms and is staring hard at Robbie. "But it seems to me that you're the freak here. What kind of person tries to kill someone for not wanting to marry them? Pathetic and disgusting."

"That's not what you said the night before you left town," Robbie says to her with a sneer and Rose's face turns red. She touches her injured eye and glares at him.

"She's right, you are pathetic and disgusting, and I'm sorry I didn't see it soon enough to get away before that jump scare of a wedding," I yell, pulling his attention back to me. To further emphasize my point, I pull the engagement ring from my pocket. Both Robbie and Rose's eyes are wide as I hold it up in front of him as if were a treat in front of one of Clive's cats, or a piece of lettuce for a circus cow.

"Give that back," Robbie snarls, coming closer so that he's standing nearby. I shift around, so that my left side comes in contact with the cool outside air and he is directly across from me, facing me just out of arm's reach.

A commotion by the lift catches our attention and I look over to see it sliding open and at least several large and intimidating men pouring from it. They are followed by the man with the clipboard, Supper, and then Snuzzle slinking after them. He collects a shaking Rose in his arms.

When I look back at Robbie, I see he has not taken his eyes off me so I take the ring in my left hand and hold it out above the abyss to our sides.

"You wouldn't dare do that," he shouts in a panic, but his eyes roam from mine to the surrounding group of people, none of which want to get too close to us as we are practically on the edge of a cliff.

"Don't get near me," I growl back at him. "Or your family ring goes over the edge, which would be a pity since this thing would probably sell for a fortune. It's probably why you came for me, right? You don't need me, but you need the cash."

Robbie licks his lips as he stares at my hand. Maybe he hadn't considered that option and this whole thing is about revenge, though I somehow doubt it. In truth, it hadn't even occurred to me at first, but had flashed through my mind in a sudden shower of brilliance, and now there's no way his desperation can't be considering it now. This ring could buy him a new future.

"Now come on now, let's back up from the ledge and we can talk about it over dinner, eh?" I hear Supper say from my side, but I don't dare turn and look at him. I can't take my eyes off Robbie because he looks like a cat who is about to pounce on its unsuspecting prey.

"Don't you dare drop that," seethes Robbie. "It's worth more than your life ever will be. You're just a pig farmer's daughter, born as a replacement bargaining chip to secure your family's future in the livestock business. You are nothing without me because you were born to be with me. Give me the ring and we can leave here together."

I can see his lies like fleas on white lace.

"You're wrong. I wasn't born for you. I was born to shine on my own!" I yell back and with as much force as I can muster, I fling the ring over the side and listen to the collected rush of released breath from our audience as the world swallows it whole.

I turn to give Robbie a grin, but he's started forward, walking towards me slowly as he skirts the open window's edge. No one has moved yet and for a moment, I'm glued to my feet, not waiting to make any movement in case I misjudge his lunge for me and fall over the side myself.

But something brushes by my leg and I look down to see that Robbie and I aren't alone on the edge. While Rose, Snuzzle and others hang back, there is one other brave soul that has crept forward without fear of myself, Robbie or the yawning abyss to our side. But maybe that's because cats always land on their feet.

It's the black and white cat Clive has been looking for and he rubs my legs with his fuzzy head before walking forward among the startled gasps of the room. His tiny little feet teetering on the edge as if it's nothing at all, and for his sake, I hope that cats really do land safely their feet. Especially if they happen to fall from ten stories in the air!

I stay as still as I possibly can, my muscles hurting from the stress of it, but Robbie gives a little jerk of his leg as if he were about to shoo the cat away from him. But, since this is the cat that has avoided capture by everyone for a long while now, he easily bounces away on nimble legs and back into the room.

But while the cat trots back towards the safety, it leaves Robbie off balance and before I can scream a warning, I watch him topple over the side and disappear over the edge.

Chapter Twenty-Two

Someone grabs my waist from behind and drags me away from the open window, but I'm too stunned to fight or move. I can only stare forward at the sky and how the horizon is the deepest orange I've ever seen. It blends upwards, turning to blood before finally becoming a purple so dark it's nearly black. Diamond stars are starting to peek out within its vast and endless sky and I wonder if one of them is the engagement ring, forever trapped among the cosmos.

The hands pull me towards the inner room and prop me up by the wall, but I still can't move because my arms and legs don't seem to work anymore. They are heavy and stuck as if they were accidentally sewn onto the wrong piece of fabric. The only thing I feel is the black and white cat as it moves to my lap and begins purring as though oblivious to just witnessing someone fall to their death. Maybe it, like me, is too stunned to think clearly.

Supper clears his throat somewhere above my head and begins barking commands to the blurry men nearby and tells them to get the open windows boarded up immediately. He then takes Snuzzle aside and they whisper urgently together, occasionally casting sideways looks in my direction.

Snuzzle kneels beside me and says something, but even though I can see his lips moving, nothing he says registers with me. Finally, he gestures for me to follow him and my legs miraculously follow his instructions and hoist me to my feet. The black and white cat hangs around, twirling around my feet and I take a chance and pick him up. He lets me hold him to my chest and I bury my face in his dusty fur. It makes us both sneeze.

"You know," Rose says, her voice so calm and controlled you'd think nothing happened at all. "You're still dressed up like a cow."

It's so ridiculous that I have to smile as I follow her inside the lift.

"Straight back to your rooms," Snuzzle tells us. "I'll have someone bring you something to eat, stay there while we take care of this."

Rose gives him a nod, but I can't figure out a response before the lift closes and begins to whisk Rose and me back to the main entrance of our floor. It feels like it bumps a slightly longer path and I almost wonder if going back through the secret passage would have been quicker.

"He's going to take care of it?" I finally ask Rose and without looking at me, she leans against the wall and closes her eyes before answering.

"It's the circus way, we take care of our own. But it's best to lie low for a while just to make sure," she says and then, with an intent glare that holds the fire I've seen in her eyes before, she adds, "Are you going to miss him?"

I think for a moment and for an absurd second, I'm reminded of Swiney Acres and the thousands of pigs who call that place home. I used to count how many went to the processing facilities every weekend, but I stopped when the numbers got too high and too bleak. Every life is precious, even Robbie's. Even if he was no better than rancid hog fat left out in the summer sun and covered in flies, and maybe I do feel bad that his life was cut short.

But he made these choices for himself and he certainly didn't need to come after me the way he did. So no, I will not miss him, but that doesn't mean I do not mourn his death.

"He didn't possess anything within him for me to miss," I say to Rose just as the lift opens and we walk out to the cluttered and noisy hallway of the Stage Girl Floor. The black and white cat stirs within my arms at the noise, but I keep hold of him.

"Well, I don't know about you, but I need a long, hot shower. I'll get that scarf for you later," she says and walks off towards her room. She waves over her shoulder before leaving to process today's events in her own way, but turns around with a laughing voice and calls out, "You should probably get changed, you're still dressed up as a cow."

"Chicken scat on a cracker, she's right," I say to the cat and he meows in reply.

I make my way down the long hallway that is back to how I remembered seeing it from before. Open doors line the walkway and friend faces poke out from them and congratulate me on an exceptional performance. One of them asks if I was around before the alarm went off and I tell her I just missed it when it started, which isn't far from the truth.

I'm almost to the door to my shared room and it's a good thing because the black and white cat has decided it no longer wants to be held and is squirming in my arms. Luckily, the door is wide open and I'm able to jump inside and kick the door shut before the cat leaps out of my arms.

"Bluebell!" Minty screams when she sees me. She hops over quickly, almost losing balance in her excitement, but Butterscotch is there and supports her before she topples me over. All three of us embrace in a bone crushing hug as the cat makes himself at home by the window and begins to groom his whiskers.

"I ran into Supper and he told us to wait here for you," Minty tells me, the worry easy to read on her face. Butterscotch pushes Minty down so she's sitting on her bed and joins her, but I find myself too jittery to sit down and stand there wringing my hands together.

"Do you know what happened?" Butterscotch asks. "Minty and I were working concessions inside the tents, but a few of Stage Girls said an alarm went off on our floor and they couldn't get back in."

Minty nods along with Butterscotch and adds, "They weren't letting anyone in or out, and then Olive, she's dating someone from Supper's security crew, said Pauly told her that June let some guy up here and he started shouting at her because he was looking for someone so she hit the alarm. But they ducked inside and didn't see what became of it."

"I... I know..." I search for words, I really do, but my emotions come bubbling to the surface and instead of relating everything that happened once Clive and I finished our performance, I start crying.

Butterscotch looks worried as if she said something that triggered it and scurries around the room looking for tissues, but Minty grabs my hand and pulls me to the bed beside her. She hugs me tightly and whispers the kind of nonsense words you mutter to someone to tell them everything will be okay, and while I don't hear what she says, I understand their deeper meaning and some of the searing hot pain in my chest begins to ease and the world becomes a little clearer.

"First things first," Minty says. "Let's get you out of this dirty costume. I'm sure you're sick of being a cow.

A small laugh bubbles up from my throat and I wipe away tears as they search through a pile of clothes and find the cutest purple dress studded with an embroidered galaxy. When I step out of the black and white suit and into the silky fabric, it feels like a welcome transformation, as if I shed my old skin and pulled on something made of twilight and stars.

"And second things... uh, second?" says Butterscotch as she pulls out a green box of cookies from under her bed. "I was saving these for later, but it seems like as good a time as any to have them."

"Have you been hiding those from me!" Minty pouts and tries to grab the box, but Butterscotch pulls them away at the last second.

"Yes, I have! You would have already eaten them all!"

"That's because they're so good," wails Minty, but she brightens when Butterscotch hands her a few and then she nibbles them with a triumphant smile.

I try to talk again, but nothing comes out so I sit there and eat cookies with the girls until the world outside the window turns dark and I know it's well into the dinner hour. I'm about to try and say something again, but there is a knock on our door. Butterscotch opens it and it's the girl with the brown hair holding three covered dishes in her hands.

"From Magenta," she sings, handing them over. "She also said 'everything's fine that ends fine,' or something like that."

"What does that mean?" I ask, finding my voice, but she shrugs.

"Your guess is as good as mine," she says before leaving. Butterscotch closes the door with a thoughtful look on her face, but Minty is way ahead of her.

"Who died?" she asks and I turn to look at her with my mouth open, but remembering my manners, I close it quickly. She's been here longer than I have, so it only makes sense she would understand this place on a deeper level. So, I take a long, deep breath and pull off the lid to the dish handed to me by Butterscotch.

"My fiancé," I tell them. Minty and Butterscotch exchange glances and sit back down with their meals.

Inside the covered dish is a pile of buttery noodles swimming in brown gravy and accented with chucks of large mushrooms. Cooked spinach is set in the corner in a small mound and there is even a hot biscuit sticky with warm honey tucked in the other corner. Minty hands me a fork and I find the words come easier with the fresh food in front of me and friends by my side.

I find myself telling them about my parents, Patrick and little Mary, and how I never want to go back to Pioneer Springs but think I may miss parts of it. Then even though Minty met Flame, I talk about her and how I wonder if she's already left to try and cross the Dusting.

I tell them about Belle and how I was born to take her place and marry Robbie, the king of chickens, and that I left him just before the wedding. That he attacked me before I got on the train and gave me the neck scar, and that he caught up with me here and tried to kill me again. But he wasn't successful and someone else killed him instead.

"Who killed him?" breaths Minty.

I point at the black and white cat and they gasp.

"Well, not actually, but he tripped over the cat and fell out the window."

"Well, it sounds like Supper and Magenta must have taken care of it then since it 'ended fine.' You should probably take that cat over to Clive, though. Snuzzle will have a fit if you keep him around here," says Minty and Butterscotch laughs in agreement. I laugh too, but find there's one more piece to my story I need to tell them.

"And then there's Milo," I continue softly. "He was my bodyguard and I thought he returned my feelings, but I was wrong. He wouldn't come with me when I asked. I miss him, but I don't think I love him anymore." I shift and pull my legs to my chest wrapping my arms around them as if by making myself small, I could downplay the magnitude of feelings crashing upon me. "He let me go when he caught up with me at the station, and that was the last time I saw him. I'm alone in the world now."

"No, you have us now," Butterscotch tells me, reaching over and taking my hand.

Minty takes my other and smiles before adding, "And the circus takes care of its own. And you also have Clive, he seems like he'll follow you off a cliff if you ask him."

"Oh, Minty, it's too soon for a joke like that," Butterscotch groans and Minty makes a face before covering her mouth with her hands, but we all break out into laughter.

And it feels good to laugh, to really lose myself in the thrill of just living and not being scared about what the future might bring my way. I thought it would be scary to be out on my own and trying to figure out how not to be only a pig heiress, but what the scarier thing is the number of choices I have now. There is a vast number of things I could do now.

I could go wherever I wanted to go. Well within reason of the route the circus takes, but I could do what I wanted to do and be who I wanted to be. My fingers itched to start creating again, to make more clothes and costumes, even if they are only ever worn by cats.

This reminds me of something else and amid the laughter of Minty trying to steal more cookies from Butterscotch, I look over to see the black and white cat staring back at me with large yellow eyes. There is someone else I need to check in with and let know I'm okay.

Chapter Twenty-Three

The black and white cat lets me bundle him in my arms once more and after promising Minty and Butterscotch I'll be back soon, I hurry with him to the nearest lift.

The hallways still thrum with activity and several of the men and women along the way stop what they're doing and offer congratulations on an excellent act. Some of them followed up by telling me I make a good cow, but none of them mentioned anything about what happened afterwards. I wonder if they know and are keeping it to themselves, but don't have much time to worry about it because the cat in my arms is struggling to get away. Luckily, we get in the lift and make our way to the Clown floor with little hissing and growling on both our parts.

The hallways here are the same glistening wood and soothing music and it takes no time at all to get to Clive's room. Realizing I can't knock with the cat in my arms, I unsuccessfully kick at it with my foot and hope he hears me.

"Need some assistance?" Joel, the tall man with the fantastic mustache says from behind me and reaches over with one of his long arms to knock on the door.

"Thank you," I mumble through a mouthful of white and black fur as the cat swishes his tail in my face.

"Anything for her royal highness, the Pig Heiress," he says with a wink before continuing down the hall with a jaunty step. I'm watching after him when the door opens and I hear Clive's sharp intake of breath.

"Found your cat!" I say with all the triumph of Mary when she would bring me the wild lizards she would catch in the stone gardens. I hope she's still catching them even if I'm not there. Maybe she'll even release them into Patrick's room instead.

"I see that," he says, relieving me of the struggling feline and bringing him inside. I follow, closing the door behind us so our new friend can't make another run for it, and watch as Clive secures the cat inside a large kennel by the bed.

"I'll be putting a tracking chip on that one before I let him loose again," he explains.

We stand there in silence for what feels like forever and the only sounds are from the various cats roaming between Clive's two rooms. I suddenly realize I'm nervous and am furious at myself for it. I've survived two attempts on my life, escaped from an arranged marriage, run through the Bleached Fields full of ghosts, and left everything I've ever known far behind me, so why I am suddenly blushing and fidgeting like a naive schoolgirl in front of Clive? I'm a Florence, and we always speak our minds. I can ask if a boy likes me or not.

"I'm glad you're okay," he says, coming to stand in front of me and oh pig's feet, he's tall and gorgeous and the way his sandy hair falls over those deep blue eyes is entrancing. He may not be able to read my thoughts like Milo once could, but I think he could one day. That is... if he is actually feeling the things for me that I am for him.

"Clive," I begin after wiping my sweating palms against the purple dress. "I, um, well..."

"Can I kiss you?" he asks suddenly, interrupting my thoughts in the most perfect way.

"Pigs in a blanket, I thought you'd never ask." I gasp, crashing into him and pressing my lips to his in a heated fury. He kisses me back just as passionately and we both stumble from the force of it, tripping and falling in a heap against the wall.

I can't help the laughter that overtakes my body when I look up at him from the floor and he gives me one of his heart melting smiles before kissing me again and again and again.

The warmth of Clive and the warm, soft feeling in my heart from my new friends beats fierce and strong within me, and in this grounded moment, I know I'll be okay. Maybe I was born as nothing but a pig heiress, but I have everything I need inside me to shine like a princess. Wait... a pig princess? Ew, not that, but being just 'Bluebell' sounds utterly perfect.

H. Marie Indigo was once a corporate supervisor for a big-time burger company, but she decided to leave and follow her true passion of writing young adult literature. She lives in mostly sunny California with her husband and four cats, and when she's not writing, she can be found inside local theme parks, playing video games or reading books while walking on her treadmill.

Follow her on Instagram: @marie.indigo.writes

Also by H. Marie Indigo
The Zamora Project
A first person, young adult dystopian romance set in an old hospice above a graveyard, a traveling circus (the same one as The Pig Heiress!) and a picturesque water park by the sea.